Charles H. (Charles Henry) Ross

The Extraordinary Adventures of a Young Lady's

Wedding-Bonnet

Charles H. (Charles Henry) Ross

The Extraordinary Adventures of a Young Lady's Wedding-Bonnet

ISBN/EAN: 9783337122300

Printed in Europe, USA, Canada, Australia, Japan

Cover: Foto ©Andreas Hilbeck / pixelio.de

More available books at **www.hansebooks.com**

THE

EXTRAORDINARY ADVENTURES

OF A

Young Lady's Wedding-Bonnet,

UP THE RHINE, OVER THE ALPS,

AND

AMONG THE ITALIAN BANDITTI.

Being an Episode in the Lives of Two Single Gentlemen.

Written and Drawn

BY

CHARLES H. ROSS,

AUTHOR OF

"TWO SINGLE GENTLEMEN," "THE ELDEST MISS SIMPSON," "THE GREAT MR. GUN,"
"JACK-ON-HIS-HEAD," "DEAD ACRE," ETC., ETC.

———————◆◆◆———————

LONDON:

WARD, LOCK, & TYLER, WARWICK HOUSE, PATERNOSTER ROW.

AND 107, DORSET STREET, SALISBURY SQUARE.

CONTENTS.

———◆◆———

THE ADVENTURES

OF

A YOUNG LADY'S WEDDING-BONNET.

CHAPTER I.

IN WHICH TWO CELEBRATED SINGLE GENTLEMEN MAKE UP THEIR MINDS TO
DO A THING AND—DON'T.

"HOMAS," said the Doctor.

"Doctor," said Thomas.

"What is your objection to Ramsgate?"

"Oh, bother Ramsgate!" said Thomas.

"If you desire it, Thomas, certainly. But why not go there again, this season?"

"Because, in the first place, we went there last time; in the second, since that fellow wrote the book about us, the whole town knows us by sight, and we should be followed by all the little boys—like tumbling chaps looking out for a pitch."

"I object to the terms 'tumbling chaps' and 'pitch'—which sound rather slangy:

otherwise, Thomas, I am inclined to agree with you. However, if not Ramsgate, will you be kind enough to say where?"

"Well, Paris."

"For how long?"

"I don't think we ought to spend a whole month at Paris, because we want air and exercise. Suppose, then, we merely look in there, on our way, and go for a tour in Switzerland?"

"By all means; but mind, Thomas, only a day in Paris. Indeed, I am sure your dear mother would not approve of our stopping any longer."

The speakers were Two Single Gentlemen: Thomas Kidd, aged twenty-one, with a sanguine temperament and freckles; and Doctor Griffin, his friend and tutor, big, bony, and very bald, whose age was seventy, or thereabouts. They were at that time at Wideawakington, in Yorkshire, at the house of Thomas's mother, and were upon the eve of packing their carpet-bags for a month's trip on the Continent.

Next day the carpet-bags were packed, and they were upon their way. The day after, they arrived in Paris. Three weeks after they were still in Paris, and they had been there all the time. Every day they had talked about going—half a dozen times their bags had been packed again, and their bills ordered; and yet they lingered! Why was this? In strict confidence, I will tell you: there was a lady in the case. Ah, you thought as much, did you? To be sure! as usual, a woman was at the bottom of all the mischief—and oh, was not she a pretty one! But stop a minute!

Why didn't I begin at the beginning, and tell the story properly? Have I not been hired to do so? Well, then: the first night that they spent in the gay capital, after a little dinner in the Palais Royal, said Thomas, "Suppose we go to the play." The Doctor said, "Yes." He suggested Racine, only Racine just then was not being played. Thomas voted that they should ask the waiter, who, when asked, said, right off, "Go and see 'The End of the World.'" They went to see "The End of the World," and the result was that they stayed three weeks in Paris.

It certainly was a wonderful performance this, that the waiter had recommended—a sort of burlesque of the events of the year. There were at least a hundred puns in it, which neither of the Single Gentlemen understood; but there was plenty of beautiful scenery, and there were quite a hundred beautiful young ladies, for whom they would not have had half eyes enough had they possessed twice their proper complement, without counting double-barrelled field-glasses of full 40 eye-power. There was a *Pas de Cocottes,*—never to be forgotten. There were young ladies with short waists and long waists, with and without hoops, in every fashion of dress, and in the fashion which prevailed before dresses were invented.

There was an ingenious gentleman who had put on his clothes, as it were, upside down, and had his arms in his trousers and his legs in his coat sleeves, with a false head fixed on at the wrong end of him; who had shoes on his hands, and gloves on his feet, and was altogether so confusingly out of shape and contrary to anatomical rules, that it made our Two Single Gentlemen quite hot and fidgetty, trying to make out what on earth he had done with his head. There were these and I cannot say how many other wonders; but above everything, there was the Follejambe! Mademoiselle—the queen of the ballet—*la reine des cocottes*—the pet of the chroniqueurs—the delight of the *fauteuilles d'orchestre* —of whom impassioned scribes had sung as wildly as he who sang years ago of the Carlotta—

> " She floated towards me from the wreathing crowd
> Of peachy nymphs, and swam—a breathing cloud—
> Less with a regulated kind of motion
> Than like a sea-bird skimming the breast of ocean.
> I thought, and said, ' In roseate light she swims,
> Guided, not lifted, by those sloping limbs,
> And seeks in Air a sister-sylph to meet,
> Whilst Earth heaves upward—sick to kiss her feet.'"

" Splendid!" cried young Tom Kidd, banging together his great hands with tremendous enthusiasm. He *had* big hands, and was very enthusiastic about many things.

"Certainly a graceful and good-looking person," said the Doctor, who was, as has been said, about seventy years of age, and a very wise old man, as will be seen.

They went home, that night, to their hotel, and partook of a light supper. As was usual with him, Doctor Griffin spent half

THE NONDESCRIPT.

an hour with a favourite classical author before retiring to rest. The last thing at night it had been his habit, for years past, to drink a tumbler full of cold water: he took it medicinally, and believed that it did him good. He had several similar notions, and lived by rule. He always folded up his night-cap exactly the same way. He could have laid his hand in the dark upon his tooth-brush without a moment's hesitation. He wound

up his watch every night at the same time almost to an instant,
and often waited for five minutes with the watch in his hand for
the instant to arrive. He was a bachelor, who had made up his
mind to remain so. In his younger days he had loved.—(Are
not the records of his hopeless passion to be found in another
volume, which I would scorn to advertise, price one shilling,
Ward, Lock, and Tyler?) Since then, he had seen the error of
that sort of thing. With regard to the follies of youth, it was
his habit to say, "Bah!" He also had been heard to say,
"Pshaw!" and is supposed to have been the only person, out of a
novel, who ever used the exclamation. Under these circumstances, how was it that, that night, after the performance of
"The End of the World," he should have had a dream, in which
the Queen of the Cocottes danced a *Pas Diabolique*, in blue satin
boots, upon his nose-end? Yet such was the fact, upon my sacred
word—as a story-teller.

THE DOCTOR'S DREAM.

CHAPTER II.

IN WHICH THE TWO SINGLE GENTLEMEN FALL VICTIMS TO A FATAL FASCINATION.

You, my dear, young, travelled friend—who have seen foreign countries and other climes, who have made your grand tour and taken your cheap one, been there and back and know all about everything, and a little more besides—have you ever seen anything more wonderful than a young Mossoo of fashion?

Truly, our own young man of fashion is a sight to be seen and thought about afterwards. The fluctuations alone in the style of collar which it is the proper thing for a young man of fashion to wear, bewilder an ill-dressed person awakening to his own benightedness. The mutton-chop whisker must necessitate a certain amount of noble self-sacrifice in one who could grow a weeper if he choose, but feels it his duty, as a loyal Briton, to adopt the mutton-chop. The first young man of fashion who starts a new cut of garment must be bold and resolute. He who first went in for the mediæval style of leg—the tight blue trouser, that is to say—deserves a monument, and my penny is ready for anyone who will open a subscription. But what is one of our young men to a "gandin" of Paris—to Amédée de Rococo, whose portrait I have the honour to submit to your polite consideration?

A member of the Jockey Club, a votary of Le Sport, an elegant, one of the ornaments of the Bois, one of those cavaliers whose fiery charger is ever on the point of running away with him—but doesn't. He kept a valet whom he could kick—the privilege being considered in his wages—and whose principal duties were to make cigarettes for his master, and pursue delicate inquiries, after the fashion of Leporello; only that there was not much danger for their fair subjects from Don Giovanni de Rococo. But he was very wonderful in his way, this French

AMÉDÉE DE ROCOCO.

young man of fashion; although not quite as hurtful to female peace of mind as he would have you believe.

It was a sight to see him strolling on the boulevard, behind the shadow of an enormous cigar. It was a sight to see him consume his daily dose of absinthe—some five or six glasses—without which stimulant he professed himself unable to get on any-

know. It was a sight to see him tossing off his four glasses of spirits after his cup of black coffee—the *chasse café*, the *gloria*, the *rincette*, and the *sur rincette*. In fact, he was a sight to see at most times, was Amédée. When he took his first breakfast in a magnificent flowered silk dressing-gown; when he strolled out for his second breakfast, in his short-tailed lounging-coat; when he took his little promenade on horseback, in his equestrian suit; and when, having dressed for dinner, he went forth and dined with a solemnity befitting so important an event. But greatest sight of all, when at the theatre of an evening, admiring the sylph-like movements of the inimitable Follejambe—whose devoted admirer he professed himself to be—with the very largest double-barrelled opera-glass money could procure.

Upon the morning after their visit to the play, our Two Single Gentlemen were seated at their hotel, when De Rococo presented himself, and made them a low bow. Hearing that they were coming to Paris, Jack Rollingstone, the fast young squire at Wideawakington, had given Tom Kidd a letter of introduction to the fashionable French gentleman, which he had left at De Rococo's residence the previous day; having found him away from home when he called. As De Rococo and his English friend Jack had spent some jolly evenings together when the latter was in Paris, he had called upon the Two Single Gentlemen without loss of time, anxious to be polite to them—expecting, perhaps, that he would find them of the Rollingstone style.

He found them, as I have said, at breakfast: the Doctor eating an egg, with a slice of bacon standing by his side; Thomas eating a slice of bacon, with an egg standing in front of him. The appearance of our friends was more substantial than elegant; and caught with their mouths full, they were, for a moment, unable to give utterance to the polite sentences with which they would, doubtless, have responded to De Rococo's courteous greeting—had they known a little more French.

Luckily for their reputation, as men of fashion, De Rococo was in a great hurry, having left his cabriolet at the hall-door, and was otherwise too much employed in keeping an eye-glass in his eye, and adjusting the points of his moustache, to take much notice of them, and had only just time to ask them where they had spent the previous evening, before he ran away again.

"We went to see 'The End of the World.'"

"Ah! it is good!" said Amédée, in English.

"It is excellent," said the Doctor; "particularly the scenery."

"Particularly Mademoiselle Follejambe!" cried Thomas, with energy.

"You think her clever?"

"Superb!" responded Thomas. "I never, in all my life, saw any one half as good." And Thomas was twenty-one, and had been to the theatre more than half a dozen times previous to this occasion.

"I shall be very happy to introduce both you gentlemen to her, if you will do me the honour of coming to supper at my apartments after the theatre is over. I expect some of the artistes whom you saw last night, Mademoiselle among the number. Excuse me if I leave you now. Good morning to you, gentlemen. *Au plaisir de vous revoir.*"

With this, the young man of fashion bowed gracefully, and retired, leaving the Doctor also bowing with much elegance, and indeed, prolonging that ceremony for some time after De Rococo had disappeared.

"Doctor," said Tom, presently, when they had resumed their breakfast, "isn't this glorious?"

"If you allude to the proposed supper-party, Thomas," replied the elder single gentleman, "I am afraid that your friend will be annoyed when we presently leave a note at his house to tell him that we cannot come. It would have been better, and, indeed, more polite on our part, had we told him at once, and, of course, I should have done so; but I regret to say, Thomas, that my knowledge of his language prevented my putting it as nicely as I could wish."

"No, but I say," cried Thomas, with a prodigiously long face, "why aren't we going? We are in no hurry about going anywhere else."

B

"Thomas," said the Doctor, firmly, but kindly, "are you aware that that young man proposed introducing us to the society of play-actors and actresses?"

"Well, but I say," pursued young Mr. Kidd, "I thought that that was the point of the thing."

"Thomas," replied the Doctor, in terrible tones, "What do you suppose your dear mother would say to it?"

By referring to the title-page of this work, it will be found to be, "The Adventures of a Young Lady's Wedding-Bonnet, up the Rhine, over the Alps, and among the Italian Banditti." It is clear, therefore, that we have a long journey to make, and much country to travel over; so, surely, you would not have half the book occupied by the description of what occurred in Paris. It is just possible that there are some evilly disposed persons who would find quite a shilling's worth of pleasure in a revelation of demi-monde mysteries, had I any to unfold. But those improper characters are here politely informed, that if they have invested a shilling with any such fallacious notion, they have been very much taken in. "What would Thomas's mother have said?" the Doctor asked. What would your mother say, and the critics, and Mrs. Grundy?

You, surely, cannot for a moment imagine that, after what had passed upon the subject, the Doctor was found that evening in the society of which he had spoken with such horror? Would it not amount almost to an insult to the reasoning faculties of the courteous reader, were I even to hint at the possibility of our Two Single Gentlemen having stopped three entire weeks in the French capital, wholly and solely, and for no other reason in the world but because Mademoiselle Follejambe asked them so to do?

From the very first moment when the writer of this narrative dipped his pen into the ink and boldly began his Chapter I. with a capital T, he was fully determined not to dwell at any length upon this, the introductory portion of his work. Why should he, then, linger over the sentimental vagaries of a young man from the country, or the doting reveries of a doctor of philosophy? What business is it of ours how many times they went to see the same play? or how often they formed part of a pleasure-party given in honour of the pretty actresses? Do you suppose, that because the writer knows for a fact that Doctor Griffin was one day seen purchasing the portrait of a certain popular performer—who shall be nameless—that he would be mean enough to make the circumstance public? Because young Mr. Thomas carried about, enveloped in tissue-paper, a kid-glove several sizes too small for him, shall the writer occupy the reader's time by idle conjecture and injurious surmises?

In short, what does it all matter to you or me why the Two Single Gentlemen stopped three weeks in Paris, unpacking and re-packing their carpet-bags ten times, at least?

Suffice it to say, there came, at last, one morning, when at the railway station, Mademoiselle Follejambe, who thus addressed the elder of our friends, smiling up into his face as she spoke, and pressing his hand the least bit in the world with a grey kid-glove, which, curiously enough, was of exactly the same size as that young Mr. Thomas treasured up in tissue-paper:

"You dear, good Doctor Griffin," she said. It was so pretty to hear her say Greeffeen, which she thought was quite the English way of doing it. "Whatever happens, you will be sure not to forget what I have told you. Mind, now; I have got your promise—I shall depend upon you. In fact, it is quite impossible that I can go to the wedding at all without it. Now good-bye, and remember I rely upon, and have every belief in your keeping your word."

Five minutes after this, a pretty head was nodding to him from the window of a first-class railway carriage, gliding swiftly out of the station. He was left there, behind some railings, peering wistfully into the far distance, where the last waggon was just visible, and now, a moment later, had passed out of sight.

He was left with the responsibility he had rashly undertaken weighing heavily upon him. Great as that responsibility was, he little thought what dangers he would have to pass through—what terrors awaited him ere he should have fulfilled the promise he had so solemnly made. Yes! he, Obadiah Griffin, doctor of philosophy and private tutor to Thomas Kidd, of Wideawakington, in the county of York, Esq., had given his word of honour that he would take charge of, and safely carry, a certain wedding-bonnet three hundred and fourteen miles upon a French railway. Rash man! The history of what befel him lies before you, ladies and gentlemen. It is an awful story!

CHAPTER III.

IN WHICH THE BONNET-BOX IS THE CAUSE OF SOME UNPLEASANTNESS.

"Why," said the Doctor, bitterly, "Does no one ever, by any chance, under any possible combination of circumstances, keep his promise? That woman Plom deserves to be hanged."

"As bad as hanged?" said Thomas, interrogatively.

"Hanged, drawn, and quartered!" replied the Doctor, with decision.

The woman Plom—otherwise Madame Plom, modiste—had certainly given her word, as a Frenchwoman, that the famous bonnet should, without fail, be delivered at the Doctor's hotel at noon on Monday; and now, on Thursday, at 12 o'clock, A.M., they were still waiting for it.

"Don't tell me, sir," the Doctor cried,—though, by the way, nobody had tried to tell him anything of the kind,—"Don't tell me, sir, that it takes a week to make a bonnet! I'd make a pair of shoes, myself, in half the time; although I should have to be taught first how to begin."

"The end of it will be—" began Thomas.

"That Mademoiselle Follejambe will have left Cologne, out of all patience, before we get there," concluded the Doctor.

"I·vote," said Thomas, "we start, whether it comes or not, by this afternoon's train."

"Without the bonnet!" cried the Doctor. "Never!"

Why should the possession of this long-coming head-covering have been so necessary to the pretty actress? No bonnet in the world, the Single Gentlemen both thought, could have been half so becoming as the butterfly-hat in which she performed in the celebrated drama that had just ceased running. A wonderful hat!—perhaps a little too eccentric for every-day wear, but which suited Mademoiselle Follejambe to a miracle.

The woman Plom, however, came that afternoon, bonnet-box in hand, and with profuse apologies. The Doctor had intended to be rather cutting to Madame Plom: he had, upon the quiet, composed a little sentence which was to wither Madame

THE BUTTERFLY HAT.

Plom, and cause her to sink into the uttermost depths of her Hessians; and there is no doubt in the world that he would have done it; only Madame Plom left the bonnet-box and her apologies with the chambermaid, and he never saw her at all.

But although Madame Plom could not be withered, they were able to start that afternoon, as Thomas had proposed, and did start, rejoicing hugely. To some extent it was a false start, and, at the very outset of the journey, they got into trouble about the bonnet-box, of which trouble here are the particulars. As there was no great crowd at the *embarcadere*, they chose their seats with care in a second-class carriage—two nice corner-seats, according to their fancy—Tom having his face to the Doctor, and his back to the engine. Then they got out their books—Tom his *Ponson du Terrail*, the Doctor his classic—and congratulated themselves upon their cleverness, at the same time that they both expressed a hope that they might have the carriage to themselves.

But hardly had the hope found expression, when two ladies and a bundle made their appearance at the doorway. Assisted in by the ever gallant man of learning, two other ladies, with carpet-bags, presented themselves. A lady and three children, with various packages, now appeared; and then a single lady with a birdcage.

"And now," thought the Doctor, squeezed very tightly into one corner, and considerably incommoded by the birdcage aforesaid, "we're full, I think."

And so they were, surely. Yet another lady stood upon the threshold and looked inquiringly round. At sight of her, Doctor Griffin very blandly touched his hat and intimated in the French tongue that the carriage had already got one more than its proper complement.

"Two more," said the lady, with a defiant sniff. She was a hard, thin lady this, who seemed to study the useful more than the ornamental in her attire, and wore a mushroom-shaped hat, a green veil, blue spectacles, buff Lisle thread gauntlets, and a gingham gown. "*Il faut descendre.*"

"*Comment ?*" said the Doctor.

"*Vous, monsieur,*" said the lady, "*descendez, s'il vous plaît, toute suite.*"

"Well, if this is French politeness, Thomas!" said the Doctor, rather ruefully, "what are we to do?"

"Get out of this carriage, both of you!" replied the lady in blue spectacles, this time speaking English. "Haven't you eyes in your head to read that it's for ladies only?"

"Good gracious me!" cried Doctor Griffin. "I'm sure I beg your pardon, ma'am—I never noticed it. Yes, certainly, ma'am; we'll get out directly. Have you got the luggage, Thomas?"

The luggage had been so very carefully stowed away, and it required so much collecting, that they were a long while about it; the fair English tourist stamping her foot with impatience the while, and a railway guard, who had come up, loading them with reproaches and ordering them, peremptorily, to make haste. There was not much time to lose, and our Two Single Gentlemen were quite out of breath when, at last, they scrambled into another carriage and dropped into their seats, nursing their effects; and, next moment, the train started.

"But, Thomas!" cried the Doctor, suddenly. "Have you—no, you haven't! Merciful goodness, Thomas, we've left the bonnet-box behind!"

Who shall describe the mental agony the travellers suffered until they reached the first station where the train stopped, or the frantic haste with which Thomas rushed down the platform and demanded the missing property at the window of the ladies' carriage?

"Something you have left!" said the severe English lady. "There is no men's luggage here."

"It is not exactly men's luggage—" began Thomas.

"*En place!*" cried the guard, gesticulating wildly.

"*S'il vous plaît—*" began Thomas.

"*En place!*" roared the guard; and Thomas, yielding to the force of circumstances, rushed back to his carriage, and scrambled in, while it was on the move.

"Why, Thomas," said his friend and tutor, "you haven't got it!"

"And never shall have it, ten to one!" cried the younger single gentleman, in a rage. "Damn the thing!"

"Thomas," said the Doctor, with severity, "I trust you will not make use of bad language."

"Oh, bad language be blowed!" cried Thomas, wiping the perspiration off his brow. "You have a turn at them yourself, and we'll see how you like it."

When the train stopped again, therefore, Doctor Griffin descended, made his bow, and smiled blandly at the other carriage-door.

"Why, bless me, there's that man again!" cried the English lady. "What on earth do you want now?"

"A bandbox, ma'am," said the Doctor, politely, but with determination.

"Whose bandbox?" inquired the lady.

"One I was taking care of."

"Where is it, pray?"

How could he tell where it was? "Somewhere under one of the seats," was the most explicit direction he could give; and how could he have ventured upon a search which resembled the game of "Hunt the Slipper"? While he was hesitating, the guard again cried out "*En place!*" adding thereto a volley of French oaths at the expense of "*ce jobard d'Anglais*" who could not sit down and be quiet.

"Well, Doctor," said Thomas, with a slight amount of irony in his tone, "how about the bonnet-box?"

"D——," began the Doctor; but just at that moment the engine screamed shrilly, and the words of wisdom were lost in a tunnel.

But if I hesitated, for want of adequate terms, in describing the feelings of our two friends, when they first found out that they had left the box behind, how can I pretend to give the faintest idea of their frame of mind when, at the next station, after some delay in getting out of the carriage—the guard having locked them in—they found the Ladies' Compartment empty, with but one exception!

"Mademoiselle!" gasped the Doctor to the exception in question—a very pretty dark-eyed one, with soft silky curls fluttering in the breeze—"*Avez vous,——*"

"*Voilà, monsieur*," said the young lady, and handed him the box.

"Thank God!" ejaculated both Single Gentlemen, simultaneously and with fervour.

"*En place, vous autres!*" yelled the guard. "*Sapreculotte—Qu'avez vous? Bigre de bigre! Nom d'un chien! Cré bleu!*"

But they had got the box, and did not care what he said to them.

It was somewhat provoking, it is true, that the train should have gone on without them, taking the rest of their luggage with it. Yet, they had got the Wedding-Bonnet, and they were happy!

"THE GUARDIAN ANGEL OF THE BONNET-BOX."

CHAPTER IV.

IN WHICH OUR TRAVELLERS ARE TAKEN, IN THE DARK, DOWN A CROOKED LANE.

Has any single gentleman reader of this true history ever travelled a hundred miles per rail, nursing on his knees a lady's bandbox?

It is not a pleasant state of things, let me tell you, to be thus occupied in the presence of unsympathizing strangers, unacquainted with the circumstances calling for such self-sacrifice. The act of nursing a bandbox does not appear to the casual observer a noble or manly act. The chaffishly inclined are apt to inquire whether that be your ordinary mode of carrying your tooth-brush and clean collar. Pretty women have been known to giggle at the sight of a male creature so employed, and the lip of the masculine stranger has been seen to curl when his eye has fallen upon the bandbox bearer. I, who write these lines, once, under peculiar circumstances (the tortures of the inquisition shall not wring them from me, rest assured, oh Artemisia!) travelled by an excursion train—horribly cheap and dangerous—more than a hundred miles, the scoff and jeer of unsympathizing strangers, nursing a lady's bonnet in a pasteboard box, because there was no place under the seat where I could put it, and they would not take charge of it in the van.

There was, in that carriage upon the French railway, no place where Doctor Griffin could put the bonnet-box he had charge of; and he and Thomas took it in turns to hold it on their knees; and their hearts were sad, and their lives a burden to them, until they reached their journey's end. But all journeys do end, somehow, with the exception, perhaps, of the Wandering Jew's. And so, at length, they came to the town of Cologne, and went straight to the Hotel Disch to ask for Mademoiselle.

Mademoiselle, however, was gone. She had waited until that morning, and then she and her party had gone on by the boat, leaving word that they would be found at the White Horse, at Ehrenbreitstein.

As the boat did not start until next day—when it started at an unreasonably early hour—our travellers asked if they could have a bed that night; but they could not. On account of some *fête* about to take place next day, the Hotel Disch was full. The Hotel du Nord and Victoria Hotel were also unable to accommodate them. They were weary of wandering. What were they to do?

"We're sure to find something," said Doctor Griffin, "and all the afternoon is before us. Suppose we dine?" They found a Hof where they could feed, and fed accordingly. There were for dinner, soup, bouilli, sausages, tongue, calf's head in batter, cutlets, kidneys, fish pudding, roast fowl, salad, stewed pears, fried pudding, and roast shoulder of mutton; having eaten which, in the order here written, our Single Gentlemen proceeded to lay aside their napkins—Doctor Griffin having said grace to himself in a whisper—when in came a round of roast beef, which, perhaps, had been forgotten; but, at any rate, it was cut up and served round in the way the rest had been, and the doctor, in amazement, saw that almost everybody partook of it.

"And, Thomas, what is there to see?" said his friend and tutor when they reached the street.

There were many things. There was the cathedral first of all, and, among other curious sights, the cases of bones belonging to St. Ursula's virgins.

"Eleven thousand of them!" said the Doctor, "bless me!"

But, perhaps, what pleased the travellers as much as anything, was what they saw in the Market Place; which was a lady who sat in a tub and knitted stockings. Yes, just exactly like Pigault-Lebrun's Rosalie, was she there seated, with an awning over her to keep off the sun, a pot of flowers and a birdcage on one side, and one of the wettest-nosed and ugliest little red-haired boys in Christendom, on the other side; to whom she was delivering a moral lecture in unintelligible gutturals.

"I wonder," said Thomas, "if she's a widow?"

"Why so?" asked his friend.

"Oh, I was only thinking," said Tom, "whether, when he was alive, her husband lived in the tub also."

"It would be rather crowded with three of them."

"Ah!"

Our Thomas was pensive for some moments. He thought that an oyster barrel would almost have been sufficient accommodation for himself and one, now far away. "I like being squeezed by girls," said Jonas Chuzzlewit.

There are, surely, some of the crookedest and most ill-smelling streets in Cologne of any town in Europe; in which ramble at large, apparently without owners, some of the most misshapen of mongrel curs. The water of the Rhine, just hereabouts, too, is rather too much of the colour of pea-soup; so, somehow, our friends were rather disappointed with things generally, and were pursuing their search for a bed in a very despondent mood, when they came upon a little incident which set them both laughing, heartily.

A very small soldier—they run uncommonly small, some of them, in these parts—standing guard over some large building, and looking very ferocious, had been chaffed by some little boys. Waxing wroth, the man of blood was for charging his assailants with his bayonet, when one of the boys' mothers—a big, bony woman, twice the size of the soldier—rushed to the rescue, and seeing her darling's danger, suddenly caught up the little soldier from behind, as though he had been a doll, and held him kicking in the air, swearing, the while, in a way which it was awful to hear. At this critical moment, however, the little soldier was in his turn rescued by six other soldiers of like dimensions, who, overcoming the huge matron, after a very gallant action, led her and the small boy captive to the fortress where, probably, a terrible fate awaited them.

"Whatever we do," said the Doctor, "we must not omit to
buy a bottle of real Eau de Cologne, and I think the best plan
will be to go direct to the manufactory."

THE LADY IN THE TUB.

They therefore made inquiries, and found that there were
between fifty and sixty places where the only real, genuine eau
was made. To one of these they went and purchased something,
which turned out afterwards to be turpentine flavoured with

musk. This ought to be a caution to future tourists; but, most
probably, it won't.

At last it was quite dark, and past nine o'clock; and yet they
had not found a bed. They were dead-beat, this time, and rather
ill-tempered, when a little fat man, with a closely-cropped head
of hair, came up and, touching his cap, offered to find them a
night's lodging "Varry goot an' chip."

MAMMA TO THE RESCUE.

"Where are they?" asked the Doctor.

"I will show," replied the little man, and led the way. He
led them down some of the most crooked of the crooked streets
the old town could produce, and stopped in the middle of one
more particularly crooked than the rest, which, though short
enough—being at most twenty houses long—had such a twist of
its own, that when they stood in the middle they could not see
either end.

One thing that both travellers noticed at the time, and com-pared notes about afterwards, was that there was not a light to be seen anywhere—neither a street lamp nor an illuminated window-blind, and that, in front of the blackest-looking house in the street, their guide had made a halt, and was ringing vigorously at a jangling bell. It was the harshest sounding and noisiest bell, too, the Doctor afterwards asserted, of all the bells he had ever heard in his life—since he heard the bell which used to ring him up in the days when he was a schoolboy at Merchant Taylors, and lodged with one of the masters in Printing House Square. But, noisy as was the sound it made, nothing came of it, and their guide had to ring again and again, and yet received no reply.

"Does any one live here?" asked the Doctor. "They must be very deaf."

"They sleeps a little bit, most like," said the guide.

"We had better go somewhere else, perhaps."

"Because why?"

"Why, we may wait half an hour, and not get in then."

"Oh, they take you in vary much when I say de word," said the guide, laughing, somewhat after the fashion of the postillion in "The Romantic Idea."

He had—this little fat man—the Single Gentlemen afterwards averred, the most murderous expression conceivable in his left eye.

CHAPTER V.

CHIEFLY DESCRIPTIVE OF A HOUSE OF MYSTERY, AND WHAT HAPPENED IN IT
WHEN THE CANDLE WENT OUT.

AT length, when the travellers' patience was well nigh exhausted, there was a sound of grating bolts, and a door opening suddenly, as it seemed to them, right in the middle of the house-side—where there was no outward sight of doorposts, step, or scraper—a man, with a sullen face, a black beard, and a dirty nightcap, presented himself, and, shading his eyes from the candle he carried, stared out at them vacantly.

To him, in a guttural tongue unknown to the travellers, but afterwards believed by them to have been German "back-slang"—that is to say, each word spelt backwards and so pronounced—the guide told his tale and introduced the wanderers. Having yawned in the faces of the Two Single Gentlemen, he of the night-cap beckoned them into the house, and the fat man with the evil eye, muttering some words in the unknown tongue, straightway—before he could be thanked or paid—took to his heels and ran away down the crooked lane.

Having stopped a moment to rebolt the doors, the man in the nightcap led them, silently, along a paved passage, took up an end of candle from a shelf, lit it at his own, and putting it into a candlestick, thrust the candlestick into Doctor Griffin's hand, and made as though he would lead the way upstairs to bed. At this juncture, however, Thomas broke the silence by observing, "I say, Doctor, aren't you rather peckish?"

"I must confess," said the Doctor, "that I am."

"Ask him for something, then," said Tom, in a tone of deep

C

injury, caused by the pangs of hunger which he suffered. "We're not going to stand him putting us to bed in this way, are we?"

"Not if we can help it, Thomas," said Doctor Griffin. "Though I do not exactly know how we can make our wants known verbally."

"Try dumb show," suggested Mr. Kidd, and the Doctor tried it.

Laying one hand upon the arm of the man with the nightcap, he opened his own mouth very widely and made three rapid dabs at it with his forefinger—a proceeding which caused the man with the nightcap to nod the same at him an equal number of times; the tassel on the nightcap adding a nod, as it were, upon its own account, at the conclusion. Then he worked his jaws vigorously, swallowed an imaginary mouthful, and rubbed his waistcoat as though he highly approved of what he had partaken of. After this pantomime, he looked towards the Doctor, who nodded violently, and towards Thomas, who did the same, and, seemingly satisfied, he laughed heartily and, turning round, walked up stairs, leaving them to follow.

"But I say," said Tom, this time more injured than ever, "aren't we going to have anything after all?"

"I have not the remotest notion," replied the Doctor.

They were, however, somewhat relieved by finding that the apartment into which their guide conducted them was not a bed-room, but, containing a long dining-table and smelling very strongly of garlic, seemed to be, as far as they could see, a *salle à manger*. I say, as far as they could see; for, according to the account given by the single gentlemen, they had every reason to believe that the room was at least an acre in extent; no signs of its walls being discoverable by the aid of the two candles that the man in the nightcap had lighted, and now placed upon the long table, at which he motioned to them to be seated.

When they were seated, the nightcapped man, retiring into dense obscurity, was heard to rattle crockery, and presently returned with a pie-dish, two plates, and some knives and forks. Retiring again into darkness and rattling glass, he came forth once more, with a bottle of wine and two tumblers; then, nodding at the travellers and smiling very widely, retreated backwards until his outline was lost in the pitch blackness surrounding it, and he became invisible and inaudible, except when, at intervals, he was heard sharpening a knife.

To this somewhat unpleasant accompaniment our friends commenced operations upon the pie-dish, which contained what Thomas describes as "the woodenest pie that ever was eaten." "And I am not at all too sure," the Doctor adds, "that it ever was meant to be eaten—at least, that is to say, the crust part."

To take inadvertently, at a strange table, a large mouthful of what you do not like, and, as you make the discovery that you do not approve of it make also the discovery that the gaze of the host is fixed upon you, is not the pleasantest situation one can imagine; but it is probably preferable to that in which the two travellers found themselves placed, while struggling with that awful pie-crust, beneath the scrutiny of an unseen eye.

"I must confess, Thomas," said the Doctor, "that my teeth are scarcely equal to this sort of exercise; but what are we to do?"

"The worst of it is," remarked Tom, "you have put so much on our plates."

"If we could only see his eye," said the Doctor, "we might, by a rapid movement, be able to return the crust to the dish, while he was looking for a moment in some other direction."

"I don't believe he ever takes his eye off us," said Tom.

"I wish he would not keep sharpening that knife so," observed Doctor Griffin.

"Why does he do it?" said Tom. "But I expect the knives want a good deal of sharpening after these pies."

The meal came to an end at length, and the travellers rose to indicate that they were ready to go to bed; whereupon the man with the nightcap became once more visible, and led them up a winding staircase and along two passages to a spacious bedroom, containing two beds, one at either end, placed close against the walls, and no kind of furniture whatever to fill some twenty square yards of space between them. And now occurred something, if possible, rather more singular than anything else which had happened since they had made acquaintance with this mysterious establishment. Hitherto, there had been a death-like silence reigning throughout the house, and in the town without; but, just at the moment they entered the bedroom, the sound of riotous mirth smote upon their ears, accompanied by the clattering of numerous feet upon the uneven stones of the roadway in the streets below; as though fiends in wooden clogs were dancing demoniacal double shuffles.

In answer to an inquiring expression of countenance on the part of Doctor Griffin, the man in the nightcap nodded his head towards the window and laughed loudly; and going to the window, threw it open and called out to the demons below; upon which the demons below responded with a howl of twenty voice-strength and retreated slowly, howling as they went. In answer to another inquiring expression of the Doctor's—which indeed was intended to take the shape of a question as to the meaning of things generally—the man in the nightcap, to the amazement of the Two Single Gentlemen, laid aside the bed-candlestick he was carrying, and going down on his knees, tapped himself on the back of the neck with his right hand. Then rising to his feet, gathered up his nightcap, which had fallen off as he hit himself, and held it out at arm's length, as though it had been the head of a traitor; after which he replaced it on his head and took up the candlestick again, and beckoned to Thomas to accompany him.

"But I say, Doctor," said Thomas, "why shouldn't I stop here?"

"As there are two beds," said Doctor Griffin, "I really can't see why you shouldn't. Suppose we put it to him?"

The putting of this knotty point by the aid of pantomime was a difficult task, but most artistically executed, though it elicited only frowns and head-shakings from the man in the nightcap, who eventually led Thomas up to one of the beds, and pulling off a counterpane, covering it, showed him that there were no sheets or blankets. Under these circumstances, and as Thomas said, "Oh, for goodness' sake, let us do what he wants—I'm dying to get to bed!" it was agreed that Mr. Kidd should permit himself to be conducted to another bed-chamber, whilst the Doctor was left alone, with three-quarters of an inch of bed-candle, and a night of terror before him.

The first thing that Doctor Griffin did when he found himself alone was to stand still and listen to the retreating footsteps of Thomas and his companion, which, after traversing what seemed to be nigh on to three-quarters of a mile of passage, were at length heard ascending some stairs, and, becoming more and more faint and distant, at last died away altogether, leaving behind a silence as of the tomb. By this time the three-quarters of an inch of candle had burnt down to half an inch, in consequence of a strong draught the candle stood in. The second thing the Doctor did was to say to himself, "I wonder what's become of Thomas." After which he examined the fastening of the door, found it in a highly unsatisfactory state, tried to barricade it with the one solitary chair that the bedroom contained, and then consulted with himself whereabouts he ought to hide his money in case of an accident; but just when he had got about half-way through the consultation, the candle began to splutter, and in a moment afterwards the wick dropped down into the fat and xepired with a fizz.

I will not go quite so far as to say that Doctor Griffin was frightened. Who would have been? Certainly, the house was of a somewhat mysterious character, and the guide who had brought them there, and the man that had opened the door to them, had their little peculiarities. Certainly, in case any unfair treatment was intended, it would have been more consoling to think that Thomas's bedroom lay within sound of a piercing shriek, should such a sound be torn, in his death-agony, from the wretched victim of the midnight assassin; but it was not. Nor would it have been any disadvantage if the Doctor's bed-chamber had only been, say ten square yards smaller; or if there had been a fastening to the door, or a blind to either window, so that the moonlight could not have poured in quite so strongly, casting fantastic shadows upon the opposite wall, on which a water-spout, outside, took the shape of a long-nosed demon peering round the corner.

The Doctor recollected, when he was a boy, having seen an

THE DOCTOR'S GOBLIN.

old German picture of a tree that flung a shadow, like a goblin sportsman, on some wooden palings, and he remembered how, until many years afterwards, when the joke slowly dawned upon him, he had always supposed that there was a goblin sportsman somewhere out of sight, whose shadow preceded him. In like fashion, it seemed impossible now to suppose that the long-nosed demon was not really there; and when the Doctor had been to the window to look out, and turned and still saw the shadow of the leering head leering over his shoulder, he bobbed back again quickly, with some idea of catching him in the act.

The moonlight, which flooded the room, illuminated the high tilted roofs of two quaint old houses opposite, connected together by a clothes-line, on which some linen, hanging out to dry, assumed spectral shapes against the dark sky. While he stood there, gazing out upon the dreary deserted street below, the sounds of more harmony struck upon his ear, and presently a straggling company of tipsy revellers came reeling by, bellowing out a discordant chorus.

A VIEW IN COLOGNE.

"I wonder how it is," thought Doctor Griffin, "that there happen to be so many bad characters out of doors to-night."

And then he added, after a pause, "I hope they are all out of doors, and I shan't mind."

It occurred to the Doctor, at this period, that he might as well go to bed. Not, of course, that that was the safest place in case of a visit from the midnight assassin, above alluded to; but there is, nevertheless, a certain feeling of security one feels with the blankets high above one's ears, as all you timid ones will secretly allow, whatever you may say in public to the contrary. The Doctor, therefore, undressed and sought his couch. The phrase, as applicable to the beds of ordinary life, I object to, nor, indeed, must it be taken in too literal a sense on the present occasion. Indeed the search was soon enough concluded, as far as the actual whereabouts of the bedstead was concerned; but a peculiarity—amusing, perhaps, under other circumstances — of the bed in question was that there was no way of getting into it.

The reader has no doubt observed that there are, among the envelopes which usually come to him by post, two sorts: one, that does not stick at all, and the other, that sticks everywhere, particularly to the enclosure, and has to be torn away in little bits, as Dundreary tore open Sam's letter. The bed the Doctor now lived in hopes of getting into was made upon the same principle: it was fastened up on both sides, and at the top and bottom.

"Though which is the top and which is t'other end," said Doctor Griffin, "is really more than I can pretend to say; for there doesn't appear to be any pillows anywhere."

The evening, however, was rather chilly, and the Doctor began to grow impatient. He, therefore, with much pains picked open one end of the bed, and making himself a pillow out of his coat, rolled up for the purpose, and rather unpleasantly knobby on account of a tin soap-box in one of the pockets, worked himself between the sheets as though he had been filling a sausage skin, and made up his mind to go to sleep. But, strange to say, although he was quite determined about the matter, he was absurdly wakeful; and, lying with his eyes wide open and fixed upon the shadow of the demon water-spout, began to ask himself what on earth the man in the nightcap could have meant by that pantomime business, in which he had knelt down and tapped his neck.

"I have it," said the Doctor, suddenly sitting up in bed as he spoke. "There's going to be a man guillotined. That's what's the meaning of the drunken people in the streets, and the hotels all being full. Dear me, how very horrible!"

This notion having once occurred to Doctor Griffin, it must be confessed that the water-spout assumed a more terrible expression than ever, and, curiously enough, the shadow of the window-frame, surrounding it, took the shape of the engine of death, with its two uprights, its cross-bar, and its slanting knife, which the Doctor felt certain would presently come down upon the demon water-spout, and slice his ugly head off. To avoid so unpleasant a spectacle, the Doctor wisely turned his back, and lay thus, listening to mysterious creakings, as of worm-eaten planks yielding beneath a stealthy footfall. Then, turning round again, he shut out the water-spout by a clever arrangement of the bed-clothes, and covered up his ears and closed his eyes.

He might have been asleep five minutes, perhaps, when he awoke again with a start, and found a man with his head in his lap, sitting upon a chair at the foot of the bed, who, as the Doctor opened his eyes, said audibly in English, "Catch!" and made as though he would have flung his head at him. Struggling up in bed to face this horrible phantom, the Doctor was much relieved to find it fade away before him into nothing more terrible than a double-breasted waistcoat and a pair of trousers, by accident somewhat fantastically grouped, on which the moon-light was playing.

Shutting his eyes again, after this discovery, the Doctor set himself resolutely to count five hundred, and fell asleep a little after he had passed three hundred and fifty.

Awaking in the morning, he found the sunlight pouring into the room instead of the moonbeams, and Thomas knocking loudly at the door.

"Doctor, doctor!"

"Hallo!"

"It's time you got up, if we are to catch the boat."

"I'll be with you in half a minute."

In little more than five minutes, at the outside, our two friends met together in the famous *salle à manger*, strangely shrunken in its dimensions since last night. Then—having had a good break-fast of most delicious coffee, hot rolls, and fresh butter—called for their bill, found it absurdly cheap, and took their departure; passing on the way to the boat beneath the clothes-line the Doctor had looked at from his bedroom-window, which, by day-light, did not look quite so terrible.

"But, Thomas," said the Doctor, three days subsequent to the events just described, "We never asked whether there was an execution after all."

"It would have been more satisfactory if we had," said Tom.

But they never did ask, and the writer is no better informed on the subject than they were.

CHAPTER VI.

SHOWING HOW THE DOCTOR WENT UP THE RHINE AND FELL INTO
A DUCK-POND.

How many times has that famous journey from Cologne to Mayence been described! and how often the legends of the Rhine recounted! Has not Lord Lytton told us the story, and Victor Hugo, and Leitch Ritchie, and Thomas Hood, and Henry Mayhew, and Mark Lemon, and George Augustus Sala; and did not a voice now hushed in death sing us his famous Rhine Song, some hundreds of times, but not once too often, in the little room at the Egyptian Hall? Do we not all know, by heart, those old, old tales; or ought we not to know them, if we don't?

Come now, reader, you recollect as well as I do how Sir Siegfried, the hardy hero of the Niebelungenlied, slew the dragon with his celebrated sword Balamung, and rescued the fair daughter of King Gilibaldus; or how the cruel young lady of the Lurleyberg lured the monk, St. Goar, to his destruction, by the sweet music of her voice.

Or how Hatto was eaten in his tower by the rats—boots and all. Or how the bad seigneur of Falkenstein cast the poor Prior into the pit beneath the turret, with his great bell dangling round his neck, the knell of which long afterwards haunted the wicked sinner in his dying moments. Or how the love-sick sister of Bertha, of Argenfels, pined away in the forest of Stromberg, where the grave into which she slowly sank—do you not remember—was pointed out to us as a proof positive of the truth of the story?

Or how the banished wife of Count Palatine lived with her child—lived in the wilderness, unseen by man, and unharmed by the beasts of prey with which it was peopled. Or how Mrs. Conrad, as Carlyle tells us, "A very pious, but fanciful, young woman," led her husband such a life that he was obliged to run away to the wars, for the sake of peace and quietness; "lodging beggars, sometimes in his very bed; continually breaking his night's rest for prayer and devotional exercises of undue length; weeping one moment, then smiling for joy the next; meandering about, capricious, melodious, weak, at the will of devout whim mainly."

Or how the old woman frightened the Devil into dropping the stone with which he would have destroyed Aix la Chapelle, and what other deeds he did and did not do; all of which are written in the handbooks of the tourists, and there may be read at length by those who know them not. It is where I, clandestinely, read them myself the night before I last made the journey; for, somehow, I had got a little bit confused as to who did one thing and who the other.

"And so this is the Rhine!" said Doctor Griffin, as he walked the deck of the steamer. "The Rhine—the Rhine of which the poet says—what does the poet say, Thomas?"

"I don't remember exactly," replied Mr. Kidd. "But I hope this fog won't last."

Upon the outset of their journey—on the way between Cologne and Bonn—it certainly struck both the travellers that there would have been rather too much fog if they had any scenery to look at. It also struck them—when the fog presently cleared off—that the banks of the Rhine, just thereabouts, were not unlike the Essex marshes; only that, now and then, there was a windmill that did not look quite English. Furthermore, it occurred to the Two Single Gentlemen that there was enough, and to spare, of a certain big bell that rang over their heads and in either ear, and generally all round them, every minute or two, and agitated them with the fear that they might lose something if they did not keep a sharp look-out. When, in due course, they came to the crags and castles, the ruins and the vineyard-covered mountains rising from the water's edge, they were as delighted, you may be sure, as you and I were when we first went up the river.

"This indeed is beautiful!" were the ever-memorable words of the philosophic Griffin. "Beautiful indeed! Grand and majestic!"

He subsequently complained of a slight headache.

"It's the scenery," said Thomas. "I feel it myself."

"Or the cabin-stairs," said the Doctor. "If you remember, there were three views during dinner, and we had to run up upon deck to see them. I presume, after a journey or two, one would get more used to it."

Our Two Single Gentlemen were not a little vexed and disappointed, on arriving at Coblenz, to find a letter waiting there to greet them in place of the pretty owner of the bonnet-box, who had gone on to Basle, where she trusted her kind friends would join her.

"At any rate, we must stop here to-night," said the Doctor, "as there is no boat on this afternoon. So the question is, what shall we do to kill the time?"

"Suppose," said Tom, with his usual enthusiasm, "we climb up to the top of the fortress, and look at the view."

"If they could only bring the view down to us," said the Doctor, looking upwards rather glumly; "or, look here, Thomas, suppose you go up, and when you come down again tell me what it's like; while, in the mean time, I take an hour's stroll across the country."

Finally that arrangement was decided upon, it being, furthermore, agreed that when Tom had done with the fortress, he should walk along the high road to Mosselweiss, in which direction the Doctor was to stroll.

"I'll carry a book with me," the Doctor said. "You be off; you need not wait while I unpack the portmanteau."

The old gentleman had brought three or four volumes with him—old favourites, well thumbed—and as he now turned them over and over, he was undecided which he should take. There was a passage in one of them he wanted most particularly to look for, and some portion of another about which he would have liked to refresh his memory, but a third was what he would rather have taken with him to read. In the end, he took all

THE DOCTOR TAKES ONE STEP TOO MANY.

three—one in his pocket, one under his arm, and the third in his hand—and, thus provided, went out for a walk.

Oh, but he was a sight to see—this learned gentleman—strolling by the road-side, with an open book held out before him, from which he recited passages, gently beating time the while with his disengaged hand; and two young Mosselweissers meeting him, opened their mouths to quite an alarming extent with astonishment, and stood gazing after him until he was lost to sight. But, while thus storing his mind with classic lore, why could our doctor not spare a little of his attention for the scene about

WHO'S THERE?

him? There are people who, when they go a long journey, will read books all the way. A capital plan, when they are the works of a certain author—who shall be nameless; but a practice that may be carried too far. At any rate, if Doctor Griffin had paid less attention to his Juvenal and more to the ground beneath his feet, he would have discovered, sooner than he did, that he had wandered off the path, and was walking into a duck-pond, lying straight before him.

But he did not discover it until he had taken a step too many, when he, Juvenal, Ovid, and Horace, all went souse in together, in the middle of a verse, to the amazement of the ducks.

When Tom came down again from the fortress, he took the road to Mosselweiss, and, failing to find his friend, returned after a weary pilgrimage to the White Horse. There, the first things he saw were the Doctor's clothes hanging before the kitchen fire; and, running upstairs, he knocked at the door of the Doctor's room. "Who's there?" cried a frightened voice, and Tom, entering, found the Doctor with his feet in hot water and a basin full of some hot mixture by his side.

"Why, gracious mercy!" said Tom. "What has happened?"

"I tubbled id a pod," replied his friend and tutor, through his nose.

"That sounds like German," it occurred to Thomas; but he thought it better not to say so.

The foregoing incident may not, perhaps, appear to a reader whose taste has been vitiated by a long course of sensational fiction, as being of a highly wrought and melodramatic character; but it was, nevertheless, the cause of some very thrilling adventures, yet to come.

The immediate result of the Doctor's ducking was, that next day he was confined to his bed, and the next day, and the next, was still held prisoner by a violent attack of influenza.

In the meanwhile, there was Mademoiselle still without her wedding-bonnet; and how could they hope that she would wait for them?

CHAPTER VII.

IN WHICH THOMAS FALLS IN LOVE, AND GETS INTO TROUBLE.

Ir is not everybody who can be handsome, but any young man may be well-dressed, if he chooses, either by paying ready money or by running bills; and, if necessary, running when the bill has stood so long, that the much-enduring party whom it represents will not stand it any longer. The sole object in life and the earthly ambition of the writer of this history—why should he be ashamed to own it?—is to adorn his person and impress his fellow man, and woman more particularly, with feelings of unbounded admiration, not unmixed with awe. It is his especial pleasure to lavish all those huge sums of money, realized by the sale of the many million copies of his celebrated volumes, upon gorgeous apparel and dazzling jewellery, which, when combined with features and figure strikingly symmetrical, very naturally attract the eyes of all beholders. The effect indeed is very imposing—(*Cartes de visite*, on application to the publishers, post free for thirteen stamps).

The young man of the name of Kidd, I regret to say, neglected many little details in his toilet, and had, ordinarily, a *tout ensemble* anything but dashing. He had money, had this young man, and was also anxious to be fashionably attired (they called it "stylish" down in his parts); but the new suit, after he had laid his money out, was hardly what could have been desired. He was, in fact, badly advised. I don't suppose there is an honester or truer-hearted man alive than Jones of Wideawakington, but he can no more make trousers than he can make legs. The patterns for waistcoat stuffs, down in that remote place, are what we

D

young bloods, up here in town, left off wearing two seasons ago,
yet Jones—(however honest one is, one must be flowery in
the way of trade)—protests he has just had them over direct
from Parry, where, he adds, winking and whispering mysteriously
—as though it were a "tip" for next year's Derby he was im-
parting to us—"they are all the go!"

Listening, in a moment of weakness, to the voice of this deceiver,
our innocent Kidd had gone in for a "fancy vest" of a check
pattern, with a check so big that on his manly form there was
only room for half of it before it was cut off short at the buttons.
He had a neat thing in scarfs, and a really noble thing in pins;
but he had not a happy knack of putting them on, so that a
deluge of blue satin generally swamped his shirt collar, and cas-
caded out over his chest. As he, somehow, never had time to
brush his hat, and was, as a rule, a day behindhand in his boot
cleaning, his appearance was anything but that of a young man
of property; and the fact of his carrying a bandbox by no means
increased the resemblance.

He did not usually carry the bandbox. There was, indeed, a
certain want of candour on our Thomas's part respecting this
piece of luggage. He allowed his senior to take care of it, watch
over it, and carry it to and fro during the journey; but he had
formed a secret resolve, of a shamefully deceitful nature, with
regard to his own course of conduct when they should have
reached the journey's end. It was then his intention to possess
himself of the famous bonnet by the exercise of diplomacy—or, if
need be, violence—and to present it to the pretty actress himself,
with a neatly turned speech, long since composed and learnt by
heart, in readiness for the blissful moment. For this underhand
behaviour Mr. Kidd pleaded, in extenuation, that the Doctor had
taken rather too much upon himself. "It was I," he afterwards
remarked to a mutual friend, "whom she told to take charge of
it. What had he got to do with the affair? Why did he mix
himself up? Some people learn nothing by experience. It is
not the first time he has made a fool of himself, I can tell you."

Neither was it the first time that our Thomas had acted with

some indiscretion in an affair of the heart.   He was of a suscep-
tible nature, and, when he was seven years old, fell in love with a
young lady in frilled trousers, next door, of the age of nine, and
very nearly kissed her under the mistletoe; only didn't, at the last
moment, because he was afraid.   Since then, other syrens had
enthralled him—notably one in curl papers, whose story has been
elsewhere told; and now it is the melancholy duty of the writer
of this narrative to have to relate how, when carrying a bonnet to

DARING ACT ON THE PART OF YOUNG MR KIDD.

the idol of his heart, he fell in love, by the way, with somebody
else.

   This somebody else was on board the steamer which conveyed
our travellers from Coblenz to Basle—a pretty Somebody, inclined
to be plump, and very showily attired.   Somebody's mamma, on
the contrary, was inclined to be spikey, and was dressed in old-
fashioned garments, full of straight creases, suggestive of many
years' hoarding in drawers and cupboards.

   There was, attached to these ladies, a boy in buttons, unmis-
takably English, who found a cause for uproarious mirth in the

personal appearance of all foreigners with whom he came in contact, and who was for ever choking himself with his fist or his pocket handkerchief, in futile endeavours to conceal his cachinnatory proceedings from the ladies. It pleased this young gentleman to mistake Mr. Kidd for a Mossoo, and a Mossoo of so preposterous an appearance, that whenever he dropped his eye

SOMEBODY ON THE BOAT.

upon our Thomas, he could scarcely stand upright, for laughing. Under these circumstances—it being equally impossible to engage with dignity in a personal encounter or totally to ignore the boy's rude conduct—Mr. Kidd thought it best to shelter himself, as much as possible, by the intervening funnel. Here, hidden from the sight of the boisterous Buttons, Thomas was able at his leisure to contemplate the lovely Somebody. But this course of conduct was not unobserved either by Somebody, Somebody's mamma, or their boy-servant, and motives were ascribed to him which, as will be seen, led to unpleasant results.

Thomas, as has been stated, was, just then, carrying the band-box, which unusual circumstance was caused by the Doctor's

SOMEBODY'S MAMMA.

having left him in charge of it while he ran, for a few moments, on shore, at one of the landing-places, to make a purchase. When he returned on board he did not observe Thomas, and went down into the cabin in search of him. Then, the boat beginning to move, and not seeing anything of the Doctor, Thomas walked to-wards the man at the wheel in search of him. Arrived at the

extreme end of the boat, he turned round again and caught sight
of Doctor Griffin coming briskly towards him, with an angry expression upon his face, and another bonnet-box in his hand.

"Why, Thomas——!"

"Why, Doctor——!"

"What the deuce——?"

"What the dickens——?"

"I thought," said the Doctor, holding up his bandbox, "that
this was ours, and that you had left it to take care of itself."

"I have never let ours go out of my hand," said Mr. Kidd;
"where did you get that from?"

"Off a heap of luggage by the funnel."

"Good gracious!" said Tom, "it belongs to those English
ladies; I noticed it myself. It's just like that affair of the
Mullyboys' black box. You'd better take it back again."

The sooner this was done the better; and away went the Doctor at a sharp trot. But as he was going down one side of the
deck, the lovely Somebody came sweeping up the other, and says
she to Thomas, "I'll trouble you, sir, for my bonnet?"

"I beg your pardon, miss," said Thomas, in great confusion,
"but this does not belong to you. It is mine."

"Your bonnet?"

"I don't exactly mean that—it doesn't really belong to me."

"I shall feel much obliged, sir," said the young lady, coldly,
"if you would give it me back, at once?"

"But, if you would allow me to explain——"

"There is no occasion for that," replied the young lady, with a
contemptuous smile. The fact was, she and her mamma, and the
boy in buttons, had long noticed Thomas hovering about their
luggage, and had, very naturally, come to the conclusion that his
intentions were felonious.

But, just at this moment, Mamma came up with the Doctor and
the other bandbox, and affairs were amicably arranged; though
poor Thomas was so confused by what had occurred that he concealed himself from Somebody, all the remainder of the journey,
downstairs in the cabin.

CHAPTER VIII.

IN WHICH THE TWO SINGLE GENTLEMEN SEE STRANGE COUNTRIES.

FROM this period the final destination of our travellers became a little wild and uncertain. There was no Mademoiselle Follejambe waiting for them at Basle, and no letter to say where she had gone. The people at the hotel were divided in their opinion as to the route the ladies had taken. The landlord said Homburg; but the chambermaid was quite certain that the Lake of Como was their destination, until something the waiter had to say respecting Mayence rather shook her conviction.

"It really is a little too bad of mademoiselle," said Doctor Griffin.

"She's leading us a nice dance," said Tom Kidd.

"This can scarcely be called a journey of pleasure."

"I call it a jolly fluke."

"My dear Thomas," said the Doctor, "Whatever may be your disappointment, pray do not use such dreadful language. The word 'jolly,' in the sense you use it, is incorrect. The word 'fluke,' if there be such a word—of which fact I am, I must confess, in ignorance—is wholly unworthy of a gentleman. Do not, I entreat you, use it again."

"Oh, that be bothered," cried Tom, rather warmly. "You're quite wrong about jolly, because Shakespeare uses it in that sense. I read all about it in *Notes and Queries*; and as for fluke, every one says fluke who ever played billiards, from Cleopatra downwards. Besides, call it what you like, it *is* a fluke, and a confounded sell, and a regular doubler-up, and no error."

"Thomas," said the Doctor, "I really cannot sit calmly by and listen to such conversation;" and he rose with something

like the expression of ontraged virtue with which Colonel New-
come stalked out of the Cyder Cellars when Captain Costegan
began his comic song.

And now our travellers began to wander, vaguely seeking
pleasure and finding little, hoping against hope that a letter would
arrive at the hotel at Basle, and be forwarded to them, and
growing, day by day, more downcast and dejected.   In this
dreadful time, among other strange places that they visited, was
the wicked town of Homburg, where the bad people play for
money at cards and dice, and the good and virtuous drink copions
draughts of vile-tasting water.   Here, Thomas pursued the latter
course, under these circumstances.   The loveliest of her scx—her
name does not transpire among the rough notcs taken of the
younger single gentleman—having made a deep impression npon
Mr. Kidd's snscoptible heart, was one day observed by him
in the act of drinking at one of the famous springs.   "If she
takes much of it, and is still so beantiful," argued Tom, "it
can't be poisonous."   And when she was gonc, he rushed forward
and got a tumblerful in (O raptnre!) the very glass the fair
one had nsed.   Who shall pictnre the smile of triumph with
which he raised the goblet to his lips?   The same talented pencil,
perhaps, might also draw for ns the very wry face he made when
he had gulped down a monthful of the noxious fluid.   "I was as
near poisoned as a toucher," he snbseqnently remarked.

But while Thomas was tasting the water, what do you suppose
had become of Doctor Griffin?   He had just stepped into the
Kursaal to have a peep at *Galignani*, and finding the newspaper
engaged, had strolled np to the table, and, jnst for once in a way,
—quite for the fun of the thing, and as nobody was looking—put
down a florin.   He had no notion where to stake his coin, and
knew no more than a babe nnborn of the rules of the game; but
as true as I am writing these lines, the very first time he laid his
money down he chose a lucky number, and won thirty-five times
the amount of his stake!

During the remainder of that day Thomas was unable to find

his friend and tutor, who in the evening was unusually silent and thoughtful; but strolling into the saloon himself next day, Mr. Kidd also approached the table, and also, just for once in a way, and quite for the fun of the thing, staked his florin; but whilst in the very act a hand was laid upon his shoulder, and the Doctor dragged him back.

"Thomas," said his friend, in great agitation, "come away, I beseech you. It is the first step to crime. You know not what you are about. The fascination of this evil spot is awful. Come away—come away."

"You speak as if you had tried," said Tom, rather astonished.

"I speak for your good, my dear boy," continued the Doctor, with deep feeling. "Once entangled in the meshes, and you will never—never——. Besides, you've backed the wrong colour, and lost."

It was true, the florin had been swallowed up by the bank, and Thomas allowed himself to be led away. He afterwards, in secret, made a further venture, but with no better success, and, from that time, pronounced the whole affair a horrid swindle.

There is nothing cures a travelling Briton of a love of play so soon as one or two of these little losses; and it is very odd, when one knows he never wished to win, but merely put down a stake or two for the fun of the thing, to see how savage he is when his florins depart from him. All right-minded persons have long ago come to the proper decision respecting the vicious games of *Roulette* and *Trente et Quarante*. Of course, when we go next to Homburg, neither the writer nor the readers of this little volume will lay their money on the green cloth. We know better, don't we?

And where did our travellers go next? Alas, there are no distinct records of their tour existing. It would appear, however, that it was in Frankfort that Thomas next fell a victim to the tender passion. Among Mr. Kidd's notes, I find the name of a concert-room, at which, according to the account there given, the entertainment is superlatively good. " Whatever you do," says

Mr. Kidd, "don't miss it. The music is lovely. The beer the best in the world. FRAULEIN SCHNAPS IS AN ANGEL." The writer begs to state that he has been to the place of entertainment recommended, where he found the music and malt liquor equally detestable. Fraulein Schnaps, who wears a good deal of dirty

FRAULEIN SCHNAPS.

book-muslin and has no voice, does not quite come up to the writer's notion of the celestial; but he may be wrong.

It was at Zurich that our travellers fell in with the pretty Miss Smith and her mamma, who had put up at the same hotel—the Hotel de Belle Vue—and here Thomas was unfortunate enough to meet with a concertina. Now he was great upon this instrument in his native town, and upon the occasion of a local concert had very much distinguished himself. He, therefore, as it was a beautiful evening, thought he would serenade Miss Smith beneath her bedroom casement.

The air he selected for this purpose was, "Home, sweet Home," of which his execution was really masterly. Unfortunately, however, he made a mistake as to Miss Smith's room, and

THE PRETTY MISS SMITH.

played, instead, beneath that of her mamma, whose maid was undressing her. As Miss Smith's mamma was sleepy, she was much annoyed, though not to the same extent as an irritable English tourist, who had gone to bed at seven, so as to get up early next morning. This person, after suffering some time in silence, went to the window with the water-jug, and softly undid the sash.

As a specimen of the unsatisfactory nature of our travellers' notes at this time, I may mention one, also made at Zurich, this time by the Doctor.   It runs thus :—

"Waited about all day to see the procession.   Didn't see much."

MISS SMITH'S MAMMA.

There is no mention of what the procession was about; but a rough sketch of Tom's gives a notion of a cocked hat in a cloud of dust having formed its leading feature.

At some place, the name of which is not given, occurred the affair of the little girl and the knocker, of which the Doctor tells

this story. She was one of the prettiest little girls he ever saw.
About seven years old, perhaps, but quite a grown-up, staid
young lady—probably an elder sister in a family where there
were babies, the nursing of which fell to her share. Or she was
an only child, may be who lived with an aged grandmother, and
had picked up some of the old lady's perk and primness. The

THE PROCESSION.

Doctor was sitting at his hotel window, and saw her come down
the street, quite stiff and stately, and mount the doorstep of a
house opposite. This house had a knocker in the English fashion,
which was very low down, and within the reach of anybody
of any height at all, but out of the reach of this little lady. To
reach it she stood upon tip-toe, and stretched forth her little
arms, and evidently strained every muscle. But alas, in vain.

"Will no one help her?" thought the Doctor. But no one was in sight. He therefore put on his hat, and crossed the road, to render his assistance. The little lady was so busy that she did not hear him coming, and he, quietly, reached over her and knocked. But when he did so, she turned, suddenly, looking at

NOT QUITE, BUT VERY NEARLY.

him with a seared stare; then suddenly dodged past and fled with wondrous speed. As, however, she did not return, and the Doctor was unable to make himself intelligible to the servant who answered his knock, the situation was rather awkward.

"I do believe," said he, when he thought the matter over afterwards, "that little slut only meant to knock and run away. I ought to have run too."

Whilst upon the subject of our travellers' wanderings, mention must certainly be made of a famous day's sport at ————, to which, nevertheless, neither gentleman has made any allusion in his note-book. The hunting of the wild boar was, I am informed, the pastime in which Doctor Griffin and his pupil purposed indulging, and they donned the most approved hunting-suits, lent to them by the landlord, for the occasion. Early in the day, how-

THE DOCTOR'S SPORT.

ever, our Doctor got separated from the party. Later in the day he returned to the hotel, looking very much knocked up, and full ten years older. He had met with one of the animals, he afterwards informed Thomas, who asked if he had a shot at him.

"Shot at what?" inquired the Doctor, in evident astonishment.

"The animal."

"Of course I didn't," said Dr. Griffin. "I probably should not have hit him, and it might have made him savage. I waited behind a tree till he walked on."

CHAPTER IX.

IN WHICH THOMAS PASSES A NIGHT OF AGONY.

THERE is a certain dismal little German-Swiss town well known to tourists, where the grass grows between the stones of the

MID DAY AT WHAT'S-ITS-NAME.

principal streets, and where a score of times at least, at midday, I have looked out of the window of the chief inn upon the public square, and seen no sign of life, except it was a certain fat dog, belonging to a baker there residing, which nineteen times of the twenty was fast asleep. The idlest dog was this which traveller ever met with; and, to this day, I have my doubts whether he would not have been too lazy to wag his tail, only while I knew him he had not got the chance, for, before I made his acquaintance, he had lost all the tail he ever had.

The adventurous tourist who has penetrated as far into the interior of this little town as the celebrated street of Skim Milk, cannot have failed to have noticed the more than celebrated pump, standing in the shadow of the church, and just before what, I believe, is the bell-ringer's cottage. This pump, I would inform you who have not paid it a visit, is, without exception, the awkwardest piece of machinery existing, and the one which necessitates the greatest possible amount of hard work with the smallest possible result. Besides this hard work, too, so much contrivance and ingenuity is demanded of a pumper who would pump and yet not lame himself that I was always under the impression that only the bell-ringer himself, who was also the oldest inhabitant of the town, could have been thoroughly master of the art; until one day I saw a little lad, not nine years old, who did it beautifully. Encouraged by this spectacle, and requested

THE CELEBRATED PUMP.

by a female native of the town, of tender years, to fill for her an earthen pitcher, I ventured upon the experiment, and narrowly escaped breaking my jawbone with the handle. At this the female native of tender years roared with laughter.

They are, in that little town, the rudest set of people I have had the misfortune to come across. It was there, on the ramparts, that I one day found a band of the town-boys plaguing an old lady and her mongrel lap-dog. In a moment of misguided chivalry I routed these boys, and rescued and restored the mongrel. She abused me for over fifteen minutes in a language I did not under-
nd, but which I believe must have been Dutch of the lowest

and doublest. While she was yet in sight, and I finally looked back before turning a far distant corner, I saw her shaking her umbrella at me, and I left her so engaged.

It was late at night when our Two Single Gentlemen reached the town, and, knowing nothing of its capabilities as regarded the accommodation of travellers, overlooked the principal inn, and sought lodgings instead at a third-rate house in a back-street,

THE OLD LADY ON THE RAMPARTS.

rejoicing in the name of the "*Lapin Blanc*," *tenu*, as the signboard said, *par E. Cocardeau.*

"It looks clean and comfortable," said Thomas, "though of the humblest."

"We don't require luxury," said the Doctor, who at the time was weary and footsore, and longed for rest. "If the people are only honest—"

"Come, I say," retorted Mr. Kidd, "You recollect that little affair at Cologne." The Doctor had weakly told his young friend the story of his fears upon that occasion. "You won't be murdered, this time, I'll guarantee. Come on!"

The Doctor came on, thus encouraged, and the Two Single Gentlemen thirty seconds later were making the acquaintance of E. Cocardeau and Madame Cocardeau, his wife. There appeared to be but one public room at the "White Rabbit," which upon this occasion was so full of tobacco smoke, that when the door was first opened, nothing could be seen of its inmates beyond Madame Cocardeau, who had opened the door and stood, just within the threshold, staring out at the travellers. But, upon their inquiring whether they could be accommodated with shelter for the night, six feet of male humanity came out of the clouds and stared at them over the landlady's shoulder.

It was not certain whether or not they could have beds, but they had better sit down while the matter was thought over, and, seats were offered them by the fire-side. There was no one else in the room but Mr. and Mrs. Cocardeau when they entered, and upon making this discovery, it occurred to our friends that if all this smoke had resulted from Mr. Cocardeau's blowing a cloud, it must have been a cloud of surprising volume he had blown. But they offered no remark, and, only too glad to get a chance of sitting down, drew two chairs near to the fire, and seated themselves in silence.

Whilst they remained thus, there was a long, whispered consultation going on outside the door—broken twice by Mr. Cocardeau poking in his head to look at them, and rolling his eye at them from round the corner. At the conclusion of the conference Mrs. Cocardeau came forward to hold a parley, Mr. Cocardeau keeping in the background and, from time to time, coughing or sniffing with much significance, as though for signals agreed upon between them. She had, she said, a few questions to ask.

"Who were they?"

"Where did they come from?"

"What made them come there?"

"How long did they mean to stop?"

The travellers would have felt somewhat indignant had these questions been addressed to them in their own country, but here they thought less of the matter, and answered to the best of their ability.

They wanted a couple of beds.

" Did they want any supper ? "

They certainly would like a mouthful of something.

" Could they eat eggs ? "

They should rather think they could, and plenty of them.

The eggs presently appeared in the shape of the most diabolically bad omelet the Two Single Gentlemen had ever tasted ; but they ate it greedily—they were so hungry—and drank with it some wine which it would be a violation of truth to say was better than red ink and water.   This rather dispiriting meal having been disposed of, they asked if they might go to bed, and were conducted upstairs, and shown into their bed-rooms.

When the door had closed upon Thomas, he found himself alone with two inches of tallow candle ; and even as he noted the limited supply of light which had been apportioned to him the wind arose, of a sudden, and, sweeping round the house, shook the crazy fastenings of the window with angry violence ; then died away again with a lengthened wail.

" A stormy night at sea," said Thomas, Kidd, aloud ; and as he made the remark, it occurred to him that other travellers, in story-books he had read, had made a somewhat similar remark, under similar circumstances, and that afterwards some dreadful things had, sometimes, befallen these travellers at road-side inns, in lonely country spots, or down back-streets in quaint old towns. As a general rule, as well as he could remember, 'twas on a dark and stormy night that these travellers usually met with their unpleasant adventures.   Was anything going to happen to him now the wind had risen ?   When he came to think of it, it certainly was a queer place—this inn they had chosen—and what signified those whispered conferences, and those mysterious nods and winks, of which he assuredly had detected several.   But the remembrance of the Doctor's night at Cologne here occurred to him, and he burst out laughing.   It was all very well for the Doctor to frighten himself with a lot of absurd notions about demon water-spouts and such like nonsense. But Thomas Kidd, Esq., of Wideawakington, was much too practical to yield to such wild illusions.

Certainly, though, when he came to look round, this bed-room they had put him into had a strangely sinister appearance. First of all, he could not understand what on earth they meant by having a four-post bedstead in a foreign country—one of those heavy funereal erections, with a dusty plume of feathers nodding at each corner—the sort of bed which, he felt certain at the first glance, several persons must have died in, and, most probably, died violent deaths. The coverlet—a piece of misplaced ingenuity in the form of patch-work—was creased and ragged, as though crooked fingers had clutched at it in their throes of agony. The woodwork of the bedstead, too, was awfully suggestive of that terrible story by Mr. Wilkie Collins, in which the top of the bed came slowly down to crush the drugged sleeper to death; and there was just such another picture as that which the man in the fatal bed lay and looked at—a sinister face under a conical hat. By Jove, who could say? Perhaps, after all, the story was not one of those wonderful fancies of Mr. Collins' fertile brain, but the real truth, and this the inn where the crime was committed. Still, upon reflection, and even more so after climbing on a chair and examining the make of the bedstead, all this was very ridiculous.

There really was nothing to be afraid of. It was not the most cheerful bed-room that one could desire, and there were, perhaps, half a dozen more cupboards, and two or three more doors leading out of it, than there was any necessity for. But what of that? You recollect the nursery rhyme:—

> " Three wise men went to sea in a tub
> If the tub had been stronger,
> My tale would have been longer."

If Mr. Kidd's candle had been longer, he probably would have prolonged his reflections. As it was, the candle beginning to flicker rather ominously, Thomas was compelled to hasten his movements, and, if truth must be told, to struggle, in almost an undignified fashion, with a brute of a boot which was rather too tight for him.

But at last he had got it off, and got into bed, and was tucked up and buried deeply down; and, considering so many people had died in it, the bed was really not so very uncomfortable as it might have been. It was so comfortable, indeed, that, somehow, he had hardly closed his eyes before he fell fast asleep. How long he had slept he had no notion, but when he woke up again, he found what he had not before noticed—that there was a window on each side of the room. He was quite certain, when he got into bed and turned, round with his back to the side he had got in at, that he had left the window behind him, but now it was on the other side, as clear as day, in the bright moonlight. However, it did not much matter to him where the window was, and he was just dosing off again when he heard a creaking noise behind him, and, opening his eyes very wide, discovered that the window in front of him was only the reflection of that at the back, of which, at that moment, a hand was stealthily undoing the sash. Thomas lay there for some time, too startled to think what he ought to do next, and watched the window open slowly. When the sash was pulled back there was a slight pause, and then, what, in the moonlight, seemed to be a human foot of enormous size, attached to an endless leg of extreme thinness, was introduced at the aperture and lunged out wildly, as though in search of a landing-place. Watching this attenuated leg, Mr. Kidd was forcibly reminded of the feelers of that awful animal M. Victor Hugo has described in his romance, and, at every lunge, in which its shadow seemed to flutter in the air, after the fashion of those toy-snakes with string hinges, he expected it would reach the bed and wind him in its clammy folds. Describing the scene, some time afterwards, in a place of safety, Thomas may, perhaps, have attributed motives to his acts which it would be rather difficult to reconcile, satisfactorily, with the course of conduct he pursued. After all, it matters little why he did so; let it suffice to say that the younger Single Gentleman sought temporary refuge beneath the bed, and lay there, quaking.

The proprietor of the leg meanwhile followed that member into the room, and stood silently, for a moment, in the middle of the floor. Thomas did not like to venture, yet awhile, upon a peep; but made certain that the robber was creeping towards the bed with upraised knife. He was, therefore, somewhat surprised, after the lapse of a few moments, to hear his visitor whistling softly to himself, and presently to hear him give a sort of fiendish chuckle, somewhat similar to the "Ha, ha!" of the second assassin one meets with in transpontine melodrama.

"He isn't a robber," thought Mr. Kidd; and then a horrible thought struck him. "An escaped lunatic, most likely. I shall have to pass the night locked up with a madman."

Decidedly his visitor must have been either insane or drunk, for after a few uncertain lurches from one end of the room to the other, he rolled himself heavily upon the bed, and began to snore, almost instantaneously. Thomas lay and listened. Now was the time to crawl out and make his escape. Now, or never! But, just when he had half thrust forth his head from under the vallance, he caught sight of another leg entering at the window. Yes, there could be no doubt of it. There was another leg. Now two—now three—now four. Two other persons had entered the room, and stood whispering together, in a murderous fashion, for a moment, then crept on tip-toe towards the bed.

Thomas's blood ran cold as he listened. The wretches were now standing over the bed. Were they searching the pockets of the sleeping man? Yes, they supposed that Thomas was the man lying there, and in the dark could not recognize him. Hush! what was that? The death-struggles of their victim? The madman was being smothered in a mistake. And now all was over. The miscreants had effected their purpose, and were stealing away again.

Thomas, listening intently, heard them drop out of the window on to some soft ground below, and steal away cautiously. When they were gone, he listened, and shuddered at the fearful silence. How could he lie there under the corpse, and wait for daybreak, and yet he could not think of venturing forth before day. And what direction was he to go in. He had no idea where the Doctor's room was situated, and, for that matter, the Doctor in all probability had been long ago assassinated. Besides, what could he do single-handed? No, the only plan was to seek for assistance.

THE PRAYER FOR MERCY.

Poor Doctor! he thought. What a horrible end to their pleasure-trip! and what a providential occurrence that he should, himself, have awakened at that critical moment! But who shall describe the horror of those long, weary hours passed beneath the bed on which the victim's corpse lay, stiff and stark, in the cold moonlight? There are cases of persons whose hair has gone grey under similar circumstances, while others have lost their reason. Thomas lived through it somehow, and with the first faint streak of dawn crawled forth cautiously, crept into his clothes, and made his escape by the window. He found it close to the

A THRILLING INCIDENT.

ground, and, by the aid of a slanting roof, beside it, easily enough dropped down into the garden.

But while he was thus engaged, a fearful noise arose within the outhouse over which he was escaping on his hands and knees—a fearful shuffling, and piercing shrieks. Without waiting another moment, he flung himself to the ground, and rushed wildly across the garden, and over a low wall, into a lane beyond. Here, at a cottage door, he saw a woman standing upon the threshold, with a broom in her hand, and running towards her fell upon his knees, and told his tale of terror in breathless gasps.

There has been a time in the lives of most of us when we would have liked to sink, as it were, down a trap, and come out at the antipodes—a moment when one would like to be very much round the corner, and come back presently—in a year or two—when everybody else had died or changed his parish. It does not follow that one need have been a very fearful miscreant to desire thus to hide one's self; and though some of you may say that this is gross exaggeration, you know very well—in your heart of hearts, as the lady-novelists have it—that it is the truth. There was such a moment in the life of our Thomas, when an hour afterwards certain explanations were made, amidst loud roars of laughter.

I have not space to tell at length all that everybody said, and how all the mystery was finally cleared up; but this is the briefest outline of the case. In the first place, the Doctor still lived, and, indeed, never was better. The person who was supposed to have been murdered had not been murdered; neither was he a lunatic. He was, instead, the son of Monsieur Cocardeau, a profligate youth who had been locked out for the night, and had come home late and climbed in at the window, rather the worse for liquor, and unacquainted with the fact that his bed-room had been let to a traveller. The persons who had come in after him were pot-companions of his, and the merry dogs had done so for the purpose of stealing his boots. When they had taken off his boots, they loosened his neck-tie, and propped up his head, in consequence of which he snored no more.

"Let's get out of this," said Thomas, when matters had been cleared. "By the way, though, I suppose that awful screaming I heard was nothing either."

Mr. Cocardeau's pig had been killed that morning. "I'd such a trouble to catch him," said Mrs. Cocardeau.

Well, our travellers still wandered. There reached them at last a letter from Mademoiselle Follejambe, naming the Queen of England Hotel, on the Lake of Como, as a rendezvous. They were then at Chiavena, to which they had worked their way *via* Munich and Innsbruck. The fair one's letter said, that early upon the day after that on which they received it she would start again on her travels, but, until then, she would wait for them. It had been nearly a week on the road, and thus, one day, late in the afternoon, they found that they had no time to lose if they wanted to catch Mademoiselle before she moved on again.

CHAPTER X.

IN WHICH THE BAND-BOX FALLS INTO BAD COMPANY.

IF they were to get to Como before nightfall, it was very certain that they must set off at once; and the question was, how were they to travel? To begin with, there was no public vehicle; and though, when first the idea was mooted, the landlord seemed to think there would not be the least trouble in the world about getting a carriage, when the necessary inquiries were made, it was found that nothing of the kind could be obtained for love or money.

Whilst these inquiries were on foot, in which apparently everybody in the village seemed to be taking an active part, and to have much to say for and against everybody else's propositions, a very dusty and dilapidated vehicle, drawn by a very sorry-looking horse, crawled slowly up the road and stopped before the inn door. For what reason nobody took any notice of the vehicle our travellers could not imagine, but they supposed it just probable that, in the heat of argument, its approach was not observed, and, therefore, the Doctor had time himself to accost the driver and obtain his consent to undertake the journey before the landlord, coming back up the village street, very hot and red in the face, said, with determination, "I have done all I can, and it is impossible that you can go!"

"But," said the Doctor, "we are going!"

"How?" asked the landlord.

"In this carriage."

"In that!" exclaimed the landlord, and shrugging his shoulders, retired, without another word, into the inn.

"I say, Doctor," observed Mr. Kidd, "I suppose it's all right, isn't it?"

"Of course it is," replied his friend and tutor, with some indignation. "The fellow is vexed because he did not manage the business himself."

"By the way," said Thomas, some minutes later, "how about brigands?"

"Brigands!" replied the Doctor, "pooh!"

"I hope so," said Thomas.

The bill paid, the travellers, half an hour later, set forth upon their journey, the hundred and one beggars of the village— apparently including all the inhabitants except the landlord and his household, who, having robbed them to the extreme limit in the way of trade, refrained from asking for a *douceur* at parting —crowded round and begged piteously. But the Two Single Gentlemen, having no small change, were compelled to turn a deaf ear to these piteous entreaties; although the most persevering among their number followed the vehicle half a mile out of the village with many touching prayers, concluding, when he found the case quite hopeless, with a withering malediction, pronouncing which, as the Doctor said, he looked quite picturesque in his rags, with his bare arm extended and his fist clenched, and the sun setting redly behind his back.

Only, somehow, although of course it was absurd to think that any harm could come to them in consequence, it was rather uncomfortable to be thus cursed at the starting-point; and as they went lower and lower down the hill-side into a dull grey valley below, and gradually lost sight of the sun and its golden rays, they, somehow, both felt a strange foreboding of coming evil, which, however, they refrained from mentioning for fear of looking ridiculous. It became, at this time, apparent that the horse, trap, and driver they had engaged were about as bad specimens of the kind as could well have been found, had you searched the whole Continent over in looking for them. The trap was certainly a trap, but of such a ricketty and dilapidated character, and so odoriferously suggestive of having also been between whiles a hen-coop, that, if they had a bad road to travel, the betting was heavily in favour of a break-down. The animal between the shafts was, no doubt, a horse, although so swaddled up in skins, and ornamented with tassels, and bells, and a fantastic harness of rotten straps and wood-work, that, beside his legs, only the extreme ends of his nose and tail were visible. It was also pretty sure that the person on the box was of the masculine gender; but it was uncertain whether he was not half blind, and pretty certain that he was nearly stone deaf, and there was no possible doubt about his being very much the worse for liquor.

There was such a jolting and jerking in the mode this melancholy turn-out had of travelling, in consequence of the wheels swaying loosely to and fro, that there seemed, every moment, a danger of the whole affair shaking to pieces, and Tom, the Doctor, and the luggage being scattered in the road. But they had no notion that there was a greater danger still of their luggage falling off the roof, until they were, in a very unpleasant manner, made aware of it, which was at the same time that they had become quite certain upon the subject of the driver's deafness.

"Thomas," said the Doctor, as they were slowly ascending a second hill, "It strikes me I heard somebody shouting."

"There's such a precious row," said Tom, "with the wheels, and the bells, and the cracking of that booby's whip, which doesn't do the least bit of good, I'm certain."

"Don't say that, Thomas," observed his friend. "The cracking of the whip is evidently half the art of driving in these parts, and if we only go as fast as this with so much of it, I should say it is probable we should stand still altogether without. But, as I said before, don't you fancy somebody is shouting?"

"I fancy there is too," said Tom, after listening for a moment; "but surely the driver must hear him, and, as he knows the language, why does he not stop, if he is told to?"

However, as the shouting still continued, our two travellers simultaneously thrust their heads out of the windows, and at the same moment caught sight of a young man in a fluffy hat holding in his hand a bandbox, and bawling with all the strength of his lungs for them to stop.

"Why, good heavens, Thomas!" gasped the Doctor, "that's the Wedding-Bonnet!"

It proved to be what Doctor Griffin had said; and having in-

THE LOST BONNET-BOX.

duced the driver to stop by reaching through one of the front windows and seizing 'him by the nape of the neck, they waited for the young man to come up with them.

"I hope to goodness the bonnet is not injured," said the Doctor; and taking the bandbox in his hand, saw, to his great relief, that it had not come unfastened. "And now what ought we to give him?"

There was some difficulty about this, because neither of them, as has before been said, had any small change. Prompted by feelings of gratitude, they would willingly have given gold, but were afraid that by so doing they might only be laughed at. They, therefore, asked the driver whether he had any silver, and, receiving a reply in the negative, looked at one another with blank faces.

"After all," said the impulsive Tom, "I don't see why we shouldn't give him this gold ten-franc piece; I am sure he has bawled loud enough to earn it."

"It is very certain," said the Doctor, "that we would willingly have given ten times the amount to recover it, if it had been lost." And so they gave the young man in the fluffy hat the gold piece, and left him open-mouthed and speechless with astonishment.

See from what trifling circumstances arise the great events of one's life! The sight of the gold in Thomas's purse, and the munificence of his donation, decided the fate of our Two Single Gentlemen. The deaf and drunk driver had sufficient command over his faculties to note what had happened, and to form his own conclusions. Peeping through the window behind him, he for the next mile or two took long stares at the Two Gentlemen, and seemed to be making his mind up about some future course of action.

"I don't like that man," said Tom. "I wonder what he's thinking about?"

"I suppose he is thinking how far he can cheat us," said the Doctor. "Nothing more."

"I hope not," said Tom. "How awfully lonely the road is, just here. And, by the bye, if he is so deaf, do you think you made him understand where we wanted to go to? Goodness knows, he may be taking us in an entirely opposite direction."

About a mile further on, they came to a melodramatic-looking village of crookedly-built houses, slipping off the side of a hill, and the driver, pleading something amiss with the harness, suggested a stoppage before a wretched-looking cabaret, round the door of

which some of the most awful scoundrels Tom had ever seen
were loafing. The something amiss required such elaborate re-
pairing, that an hour had passed away before there seemed any
likelihood of the affair reaching a happy conclusion.

There was now no sign remaining of the setting sun, and the
gray shades of evening were fast gathering round them; upon dis-
covering which the Doctor indignantly inquired how much longer
they were likely to be detained? The driver, shaking his black
locks and peering up under his black eyebrows at his questioner,
replied only by a smile and a shrug of his shoulders, at which
both gentlemen waxing very wroth, they at last contrived, by
dint of threats, which they rendered as intelligible as their
knowledge of Italian permitted, and the use of the words
"*Presto sacremento,*"—which they had reason to believe meant
"Look sharp," with bad language—to get upon the road
again.

This, however, was not done without changing a golden
piece, to pay for the horse's bait and some very bad wine which
they had thought themselves called upon to order, but could not
drink; and the awful scoundrels all gathered round in order to
peep into the Doctor's purse, and exchanged various winks and
nudges among themselves.

"I can't say I altogether like this journey," observed Tom, as
they drove slowly away. "I hope we shan't come to grief."

"We should be pretty certain to come to grief, as you call it,"
replied the Doctor, snappishly, "if we stopped where we were.
We should never have left that village with our lives, if we had
been rash enough to stop there all night."

"I wish we were at Como," said Tom, "that's all."

They jogged and jolted onwards for another hour, and now
night had fully set in, and the moon had risen and was shining
brightly upon the fir trees shading them. They had just
reached a wild and secluded spot, where a hanging wood was on
one side of them and a deep precipice on the other.

"Bless me!" said the Doctor, looking out upon the precipice
side, "I hope the horse won't stumble till we get on a little

F

further. How quiet it is too! I don't believe there is another soul within a mile of us."

The Elder Gentleman was somewhat incorrect in this idea, as the events of the next moment proved, for scarcely had he ceased speaking, when a sudden shrill whistle struck upon the travellers' ears, and, simultaneously popping their heads out of the windows, they beheld some eight or nine men draw up in a line across the road, each carrying a long-barrelled gun, which he pointed at the carriage; under which alarming circumstances the Doctor and his pupil drew in their heads again, much quicker than they had thrust them out, and regarded one another with long faces.

"It is the bandits," said Thomas. "What the deuce are we to do?"

"Nothing," replied the Doctor. "What'll they do?—that's the question."

The driver's terrified exclamation of "*I ladri!*" was not wanted to indicate the character of the strangers. Black-muzzled rascals were they, to a man; and though not quite as picturesque as our operatic version of "Fra Diavolo," they had something of the stage-dress about them, with, as it were, modern improvements here and there in the shape of a hat, or an over-coat, or a fancy waistcoat, suggestive of robbed and murdered travellers.

"Oh dear!" groaned the Doctor. "What very determined-looking miscreants." And, before he had time to say more, the door on his side was pulled open, and the foremost of the bandits, grasping the old gentleman by the coat-collar, dragged him roughly out into the road, where, as he sat in the dust, another bandit placed the muzzle of a gun to his ear and cheerfully clicked the trigger.

With his mind fully made up that his earthly career would terminate in the course of the next minute or two, Doctor Griffin closed his eyes and waited patiently. In the meantime, Tom was dragged out of the carriage, and flung down like an old pair of shoes.

They were rather unnecessarily violent, these romantic ruffians, and the sight of the many pistols and poignards stuck about their persons was far from assuring.   Even with the carriage they were rather rougher than they need have been, for not only did they go inside, tear down all the lining and smash up the seats, but they broke the shafts, cut the horse loose from its complicated harness, and dragging the crazy old trap to the edge of the ravine, pushed it over—to fall crashing and clattering, through the brushwood, down into the dizzy depths below.

This disposed of, they turned their attention to the business of searching the captives and their luggage.   First, the Doctor's pockets were turned inside out; and one in which a favourite author had got, somehow, tightly wedged, was sliced open by a dagger-knife to save time, and its contents being found to consist only of two favourite volumes and nothing else, were ruthlessly flung away down the ravine.

The Doctor's famous silver repeater—a wonderful piece of workmanship, in the manufacture of which the maker had not stinted himself for room—was hauled violently out of his fob, and immediately thrust into the girdle of one of the banditti; while, at the same time, another appropriated the Doctor's double eye-glass, and set it astride of his own nose: at which piece of facetiousness the other robbers laughed loudly.

They were evidently jolly dogs, in their way—these felonious gentlemen—though it was somewhat difficult for our two friends, just at this moment, to enter into the spirit of the thing.   As though anxious to bring the point of their jokes to the notice of the captives, the bandits, in a waggish sort of way, set to nudging them in the ribs and probing them in the back, and, indeed, all parts of their body where anything like a purse or a pocket-book might, by chance, be concealed.   Our Thomas, who, under ordinary circumstances, was very ticklish, and would have roared with hysterical laughter under this manipulation, at present, somehow, did not feel inclined even to smile.

They found, sure enough, a dozen or so napoleons in a purse upon the Doctor, and half a dozen on Thomas.   In the latter's coat-pocket they also found a pocket-book, containing the Two Single Gentlemen's passport; but these discoveries did not seem to satisfy the robbers.

"Where are your effects?" asked the most ferocious, in broken French. "Quick, quick—your money!"

"Thomas," said the Doctor, in a faint voice. He was lying on his back at the time, and, by rolling his eye round at an acute angle, just managed to catch a glimpse of his companion. "Thomas, if you can think of the French for it, tell them we are robbed as much as we can be."

"There's a scoundrel got his knee in my back, and I can't think of anything," replied Mr. Kidd.

"So you won't speak, either of you," continued the ferocious brigand who had before spoken. "Very well—we'll take care of you till you change your minds, or your friends buy you off. You shall have writing materials before you go to bed. Come along!"

The Two Gentlemen found themselves, next minute, jerked upwards, and stood staring one at the other helplessly. Before, however, they had time to exchange a word, they were marched off in separate directions, and each tied to a tree, whilst the bandits amused themselves with the luggage. It was, you may be sure, a cruel sight to the poor Doctor to see his classic authors handed about with grossly disparaging remarks; and not the pleasantest thing in the world to see the various articles of his wearing apparel held up, one by one, for general inspection, and thrown back into the portmanteau with expressions of a derisive character with regard to their make and texture. There was, in particular, one pair of stockings, which certainly had been darned to the last extremity—a piece of elaborate needlework, highly praiseworthy, yet of a nature of which their proprietor would scarcely desire to make a public exhibition.

Then came Thomas's little store, among which was the kid-glove before-mentioned, wrapped up carefully in half a dozen papers, the unwrapping of which half a dozen of the brigands stood round to watch with intense eagerness, all swearing, simultaneously, a tremendous oath when they reached the hidden treasure, and found it to be what it was.

But, worst of all, was when the sacred band-box was laid violent hands on, and sacrilegious fingers, tearing away the silver paper in which it was enveloped, the loveliest little fly-away, coquettish bonnet human eyes ever looked upon stood revealed. At sight of this, the bandits set up a shout, and one black-muzzled miscreant, actually putting it on to his great bullet-head, danced round, with a bear-like agility, in what he intended to be a waltz step.

This terpsichorean feat was brought to a close by the ferocious bandit, who appeared to be the chief of the party, giving the order to move on. The things were, therefore, hastily thrown back into the portmanteau, and the captives loosened from their bondage. Closely guarded, then, the Two Single Gentlemen were marched away in opposite directions, and while turning his head to cast one long wistful glance towards his unhappy pupil, the poor Doctor took what he thought was very probably the last glimpse he should have of him upon earth, and, next moment, found himself in pitchy darkness.

CHAPTER XI.

IN WHICH MR. WILKINS LOSES HIS BREATH.

THE fact was, that the robbers had taken him into their cave. It was not exactly the sort of cave one is led to believe robbers usually live in, being rather limited as regarded space—it was about five feet by seven—and uncommonly unpleasant as regarded smell.

Before the writer of this history was in his teens, and when he went to a genteel day-school in one of the western suburbs, he and another boy, one memorable half-holiday, began to dig a cave in the other boy's papa's back-garden. It was not a sudden idea by any means. On the contrary, it had been well thought over for some weeks previously Plans had been drawn upon a slate —during school hours, and under the shelter of a dictionary placed on end between the artist and the tutor who had charge of us —and we were quite settled upon several important details. There were to be barrels of gunpowder—a dozen or two. There were to be ladders connecting one floor with another; and there were to be any number of swords, and pistols, and flasks of brandy. I cannot exactly remember—after this lapse of time— how these things were to be got together, but that is of no consequence; anyhow they *were* to be got, and one half-holiday we began to dig the hole. We had only one spade between us, and I recollect that we were both most anxious to be the first to use it. Eventually we tossed up, and the other boy—he was always the lucky one—won and went in.

All this happened so long ago I can hardly be expected to recollect much about it; but I think I may fearlessly state that there never was in all the world a harder bit of ground, or one so larded with brick-ends, as that brute of a garden of the other boy's papa's; and I don't believe a spade was ever manufactured which could have got through it. When we were drawing the plans, we had both agreed that the cave must be twenty feet deep at least. Then, when we had got down so far, we were to scoop out passages and dining-rooms, and so on. A third boy at our school, on hearing these details, said, " What will you do when you've done it ?" Upon this, the other boy—the one who was going into the underground business—replied, right off, " We shall carouse !" The idea that it would be no end of an awful jolly lark, carousing when we got down a little deeper, lent considerable animation to the first twenty spadefuls. After that there was some flagging, and the other boy's papa happening to come home, rather unexpectedly, and not entering into the affair as he ought to have done, he made us fill the hole up again. Since then I have not done much in the cave way.

The Doctor, left to himself in this cavernous apartment, which nature had formed in a rock, sat down upon a broken box he found there, and nursed his knees; as the little boys do upon a river's bank before they bathe, and ask their friends in the water whether it is cold.

"This is very awful," he thought. "What will Thomas's mother say when she gets our letter ? Indeed, the question is, will she ever get it ? And if she doesn't, what will become of us ?"

Dreadful visions arose before the poor gentleman's mind's eye as he made this reflection. He had heard stories of a captive's teeth being sent, one by one, to his friends, with a toe-nail, now and then, by way of variety. And, after all he had suffered for its sake, the Wedding-Bonnet would never reach its owner!

The ferocious bandit, before leaving him, had sworn in French for several minutes, and had shaken his gun in the Doctor's face, which the latter took as hints that he had better not attempt to escape; but, after two or three hours had elapsed without seeing or hearing anything of any of the band, he began to suppose that the letter about which they had spoken would not be demanded

of him until next day.   Immensely relieved by this idea, and not
without a faint hope that help of some sort might arrive in the
interval, the Doctor, still sitting on his box, and still nursing his
knees, closed his eyes and thought he would venture upon a
nap.

THE DOCTOR'S FLIGHT.

He soon awoke, however, when all but tumbling off his seat, and
sat bolt upright to listen.   It was awfully dark, and very still.
He could not hear a soul stirring, and creeping to the entrance,
listened, and crept back again and took another nap.

This time he really did tumble; so, getting up again, he arranged
his seat in a corner against the wall, and turning up his coat-
collar with a dread of waking up presently to find a toad or

two had crept into his trousers' pockets—as he had read was the case with some one who once fell down an old coal-pit—he went fast to sleep.

When he awoke again it was no longer so dark.

He crept cautiously to the doorway, and peeped out. It was

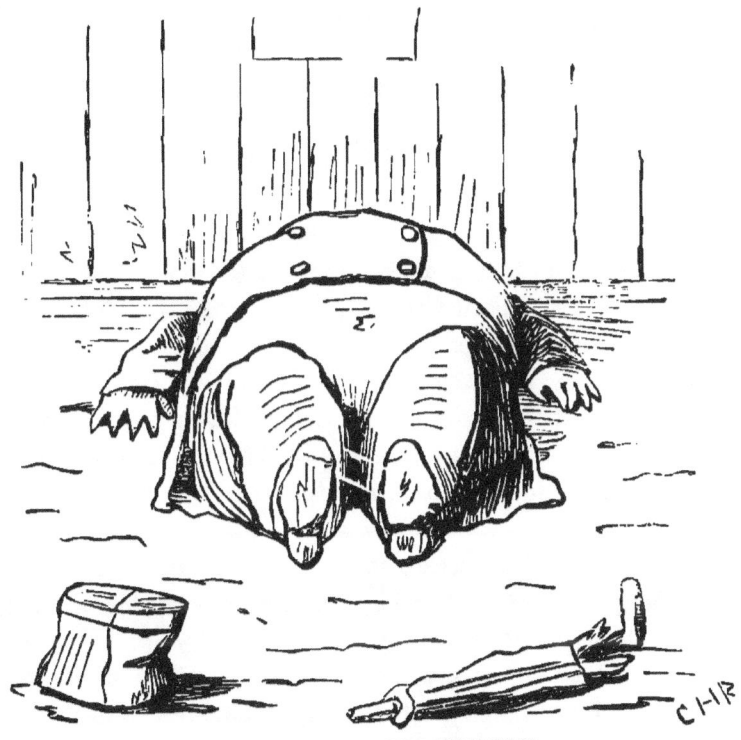

THE RESULTS OF THE COLLISION.

daylight, and all was as still as it had been when he listened before.

"I wonder," said the Doctor to himself, "whether I could see anything of Thomas."

Why should he not venture? He could see no sentry. If he walked on tip-toe, and held his breath, he might be able to re-connoitre.

He was not very well up in the exciting fictions of J. Fenimore, but he had some vague recollection of a person of the name of Hawkeye making his escape out of an Indian encampment.

"I'm not quite certain now," he thought, "but I rather fancy he did a good deal by crawling on his stomach. It was also a great point with him—if I am not mistaken—to get to windwards of the enemy, and also to cut off the trail by wading up a stream. I almost wish I had paid more attention to the subject when I had a chance. I'll buy the whole series, if I ever get home again. I think they're only sixpence each."

He crept out a little further still, until he was free of the cave, and yet could see nothing of the robbers.

But he saw, right in front of him, at the foot of a tree, the bonnet-box that had been the cause of all his troubles, lying by the side of his portmanteau.

What, however, had become of the bandits? He stood still to listen, and peered anxiously round, but could, as yet, hear and see nothing of them. To the right, round the rock, the road seemed perfectly clear. Suppose he were to seize the bonnet-box and run for his life?

It was a wild and desperate scheme; but it was worth risking. If they caught him, they would certainly have all his teeth out; but yet he thought he would venture. Hawkeye probably would have wriggled away like a worm, or crawled off in a bear-skin; our Doctor of philosophy, after some moments' reflection, determined upon taking to his heels, and took to them.

He had hardly started, however, when he heard a shout. He had, in this moment of terror, a sort of notion that Hawkeye would have lain down, so that the shots might go over him; but he thought he would not risk that course of action, and so ran faster than before. There were no shots, but the shouting continued, and grew louder, and he also heard the sound of feet in pursuit. Then, setting his teeth, he ran like mad.

For a hundred yards he urged on his wild career without stopping or looking round, and by this time had reached a wind of the road, and, turning the corner, he ran, full butt, at a fat man carrying an umbrella, and laid him, as well as himself, flat by the violent concussion.

Giving himself up for lost, the Doctor lay here in the dust, and listened to the shouts of his pursuer, which grew nearer and nearer, until at length he recognized his young friend Thomas's voice, and the words, "Hold hard, I say; what the devil are you running for?"

Upon this the Doctor sat up, and looked about him. There lay the fat man where he had fallen—probably dead; there lay his umbrella, and there also was the famous bonnet-box, smashed out of all shape.

"Good heavens!" said the Doctor, "after all I've gone through the bonnet's spoilt."

"No, it isn't," Thomas said, when he presently arrived, carrying a paper parcel in his hand. "That's only the box you ran away with. I found the bonnet hanging in a tree, where they had put and forgotten it."

"Where are they?" asked the Doctor, getting on his feet. "Let us lose no time—they will follow us directly."

"Not they," said Mr. Kidd. "It's my opinion they left us early last night. Where did they put you? I was thrust into a beastly hole, as dark as pitch, and one of the robbers threatened to murder me if I as much as winked. I waited all night, watching and listening, but could see or hear nothing, and at daybreak I crept out and looked round, and there was not a sign of a bandit to be seen."

"By the way," said the Doctor, "who's our fat friend?"

They picked up the stout gentleman, who was, by this time, recovering his breath, and assisted him to a rustic seat outside a quaint little wooden chapel, in front of which the collision had taken place.

When he was able to speak, he said his name was Wilkins, and that he was an Englishman travelling for pleasure. He added that he had not had much pleasure so far. Upon hearing that the two travellers had just escaped from bandits, he said he thought he would turn back with them to the village at the bottom of the hill. As they walked along, he said to the Doctor, " Perhaps you would be so good as to go first when we come to a corner. Some one else might be running away, you know. I don't think I could take two of those shocks, before breakfast. Have you ever been to one of the swimming-baths in Paris?—cramfull they are sometimes—reminds one of shrimp sauce. I tried to float there once, and a fellow took a header right into me. There's few things knock more of the wind out of you than that does."

THE SENSATION HEADER.

CHAPTER XII.

IN WHICH THE TWO SINGLE GENTLEMEN ARE LOST IN THE SNOW.

Of course she had gone.

IN THE TUILLERIES.

"How long ago?" asked the Doctor, of the landlord of the
Queen of England Hotel.

Circumstances had occurred, the landlord somewhat vaguely

explained, which had caused the lady to alter her plan. Instead of starting that morning she had started over-night.

"And where, in heaven's name, has she gone to now ?"

To this inquiry the landlord shrugged his shoulders. There was, however, he believed, a note for Monsieur, which might explain. Why had he not said so before ? He could not say. Well, no matter. Let the letter be produced. Ah! there it was at last. Now, what did *it* say ?

"Oh, you dear, good Doctor Griffin," said the letter,—it was on pink paper, delicately scented,—"Whatever can you think of me ? And after all the trouble I have given you. But you are so good ! so GOOD ! I was compelled to go before the time. We are to cross the Alps early to-morrow. Now, you must come. You will find us at the Convent, and there I hope to relieve you of your charge. Oh! how can I ever sufficiently thank you ?"

As if he wanted any thanks ! What was there in what he had done to make such a fuss about ? What were a few hundred miles more or less ? Nothing, a mere nothing ; nothing at all, absolutely !

While he was reading this dear letter the time slipped away in a most unaccountable manner, and Tom, who was kicking his heels outside, lost all patience, and presently came in, fuming wrathfully, to know what on earth was the matter ?

Ah! what follies do we not all, old and young, commit under the influence of the master passion ? but the old ones are ever so much the worse. Now, here was a doctor of philosophy, a person of mature age, accustomed to the instruction of youth ; in whose mouth the words of wisdom were as plentiful as blackberries are in country lanes during the blackberry season. How often had he roared with laughter at the absurdities which people in love committed ! When he was in Paris, it was he who had been so indignant in the Tuilleries Gardens at the scandalous way in which the nursemaids neglect their young charges to make love to the Tourlourous. "Outrageous sluts !" he had observed, with virtuous indignation. "But nobody thinks of anything else in this place," he said upon another occasion. "Look at their plays, and books, and pictures. Look at—at everything. Oh! I have no patience with them. Bah!" But the remarks above quoted were not made during his last visit, but long ago, and to Mrs. Kidd, our Thomas's dear mother.

Alas! what a change was there since then in one who had been so far above reproach—so solemn—so profoundly philosophical —such a splendid classical scholar, with such a head for mathematics, and a memory for Greek participles, seldom, if ever, equalled. And all upon account of that little Mademoiselle from the French playhouse! I feel certain that all young ladies who may read this volume will agree with the writer that nothing could have been more ridiculous.

"She has gone on," he said to Tom.

"Oh, of course," said Tom, bitterly; "where to next? Australia?"

"Not quite as bad as that; still, bad enough."

"I suppose we must follow again in the old style."

"My dear boy, I am afraid we are acting in a manner which, to a third person, would appear to be extremely unwise."

"There's very little doubt about that; but I don't see what it matters."

"What it matters, Thomas! I cannot admire this tone of recklessness—though, as you no doubt intend your words to mean, we have only ourselves to please; that is to say, there is only your wish to be consulted. Shall we, therefore, go up the St. Bernard?"

"We might as well go there as anywhere else."

"I understand it is a place well deserving a visit."

"Oh! I've heard so myself, often."

"Besides, it is decidedly our nearest way home."

"Oh, decidedly!"

A little later on, they spoke upon the subject to their new acquaintance, Mr. Wilkins, who had accompanied them to Como, and asked which way he was going?

" I've no notion," he replied.

" Will you come with us, then ?"

" I don't see why not. Come on."

He seemed to think that they should start that very moment, without the slightest preparation, and walk straight ahead. Upon inquiry it turned out his only luggage was his purse, a penknife, and a toothbrush.

" I bought a railway guide when I started," he said, " but I soon chucked it away; it was such a nuisance dragging it about. What's the good of a holiday if you work in it ?"

" But how do you do about clean linen ?" asked Tom.

" I buy shirts, collars, socks, and such like, when I want them, and leave the old ones at the hotel. Sometimes they make me an allowance. When they bring the bill, you know, I say, 'How many francs? Oh! so and so, is it? Well, there's a couple of shirts to come out of that. How much do you make that come to ?' They're a little surprised at first, but, after a little talk, they come to see the point of it."

" I wonder, now," said Doctor Griffin, when the three gentlemen arrived at the Hotel de la Tour, at Martigny, " if we could get a vehicle to take us up the mountain."

" There are things called Charry Bangs," said Mr. Wilkins, " and if you want to be well shaken before taken you'd better try one : they're a sort of cross between a four-post bedstead and a costermonger's barrow, with a faint notion of a jaunting-car and a half-suspicion of a Hansom cab, with part of the knife-board of an omnibus stuck on sideways round the corner. Do you understand ?"

" Not exactly," said the Doctor, looking very solemn.

" I haven't got a pencil with me, or else you might work it out on a bit of paper. Threes in two don't go, so carry it yourself, and nothing over."

They started at six in the morning, after a capital breakfast of honey, coffee, bread and cheese, and wine, and tramped along for several miles without meeting with any object of great interest in

the surrounding scenery, which was, for the most part, composed
of overhanging granite rocks.

About midday they stopped at Orsières for lunch, and had
some *œufs sur le plat*, cooked as eggs can only be cooked on
the Great St. Bernard, and some most delicious cutlets, washed
down by some very good wine.   As Mr. Wilkins was more than

ONE WAY OF GOING UP A MOUNTAIN.

ordinarily facetious, the meal was somehow prolonged beyond the
time they had at first contemplated spending over it, and the
day was well advanced when they again set forth upon their
journey.

" Somehow, one doesn't feel so springy after one has had a
tightener of that character," said Mr. Wilkins.   " I once went up
a mountain, somewhere abroad,—but I never can think of their
crack-jaw names,—with an English lady, who rode all the way on

G

the guide's back. Not à la vivandière," he added, hastily; "on a saddle-chair, you know, such as they fix on the donkeys' backs at Hampstead for little babies."

It turned out in the end, much to the travellers' surprise, that their friend Mr. Wilkins, who somehow at first they had both mistaken for a Cook's excursionist upon his first tour, had been almost everywhere, and when cross-examined, knew something upon every subject broached. It was a pleasant fancy of his to pronounce foreign words as they were spelt in English; but whether this was a joke or an artful way of escaping from committing himself by an attempt at the right pronunciation, it was rather difficult to decide. Upon this plan, Boulogne with him was not Bouloine, as some of us are pleased to call it, but Bou-logg-ny, with the emphasis on the g. A café he made to rhyme with safe, and a double meaning was, upon the same principle, a Dublin tender. But he certainly was wonderful company, and kept our friends in a roar the whole journey, as he has often enough done with other company; for he is a real flesh-and-blood traveller I am sketching, who actually did go up the St. Bernard last summer —although, by the way, his name is no more Wilkins than mine is.

Unfortunately, as it turned out in the end, our tourists spent so much time at Orsières, and afterwards loitered so long upon the road, that they were left full two miles behind a party of travellers, in char-à-bancs and on foot, whom they at first had taken as a sort of guide during the ascent.

The scenery was, indeed, so beautiful that they might be forgiven if they loitered some time to admire the picturesque little châlets, dotted on the mountain-side, half hidden by clinging grape-vines. Presently, they came in view of the lovely valley in which lies the village of Dranse. A broad expanse of rich pasture-land spread out before them, merged in the far distance in the reddish-brown of the mountain. The faintly-heard roaring of the river, mingled with the tinkling of the cattle-bells, whilst, every now and then, was heard the long, clear note of the cow-boys' Ranz des Vaches. Above them reared its head grandly the snow-topped mountain, upon which they could just trace the zig-zag line of the path they were to travel.

"Talk about the far-distant climbs," said Mr. Wilkins, "you've been up the Riggy, I suppose? That's where they go, you know, to see the sun rise. Best to let him rise by himself, I think, and wait till he's shaved and read the paper before you look at him. I've seen him, coming home of a morning, when I've been out late at my Bible-class; he's too hard and grey for my taste. I'm like what's his name, who preferred the day when the chill had been taken off. But everybody gets up on the Riggy; it's the only thing you go for, and you go to bed by daylight the day before, so as to be sure to do it; only there never was such an inn, even in Paris, for noise, and you never get a wink through the night. You know how they go on at a foreign hotel, ringing bells and dropping wooden shoes out of the fourth story into the court-yard. It's ten times worse, though, up the Riggy. They seem to keep the mules and the muleteers in the parlour, and they're always jostling one another like the chickens in a hen-house. That (the hen-house) must be the most trying place to get a sleep in I know of. You stand on one leg, you know, with your head under your wing, and some one gives you a shove when you're dozing."

As they arrived at the last village on the mountain, the glow of the afternoon sun had faded, and big drops of rain began to fall. The scenery around them was wild and savage, and a low wailing wind sweeping over the mountain-side, seemed to threaten the coming of a storm.

"I hope we shall not have bad weather," said the Doctor.

"Perhaps we had better put up here for the night, if they can give us a shake-down," suggested Mr. Wilkins.

But Thomas, sanguine and impetuous as ever, said, "No; let's push a-head."

"Whatever you like," said Mr. Wilkins; "the top of this hill seems to have a trick of getting a little further off the higher you get up; but, perhaps, that's the fun of the thing."

A mile away from the village the rain began to fall heavily, and, as they got still further up, changed to a blinding sleet, drifting right into their faces, with, at the same time, as Mr. Wilkins said, a disposition to get round the corner into the nape of their necks. The scene before them was awfully still and dreary, and no sign of life was visible, save one faint glimmering light in the window of a lonely hut, called the Canteen."

"It's only three miles more," said Tom, after making inquiries; "and look here, they've lent us a lantern."

"Good heavens! Thomas," cried the Doctor, "you must be mad to think we can go on any further. Let's sleep here."

"Well, I'm wet through," observed Mr. Kidd, "and you are not far off it, I suppose. How about rheumatism? Besides, if we don't get there to-night, she will be gone again, I suppose."

They still had that everlasting band-box in their company. They had left the portmanteau at Martigny, with directions that it should be forwarded next day, but the bonnet they had decided upon taking with them, and the Doctor and Thomas, by turns, shared the honour of its guardianship.

"Well, let's get on—if Mr. Wilkins is agreeable?" said the Doctor, after a pause.

"By all means," said their cheerful companion; and on they tramped.

But this was a rash conclusion to arrive at, as they found to their cost a mile or two further on. The sleet had now changed to snow, which in some places almost obliterated all traces of the path they had to follow, and icy flakes dashed into their faces with such violence that they expected every moment to be blinded by them. Now and again lurid glares of lightning lent a demoniacal grandeur to the savage wildness surrounding them, whilst the howling of the wind was a more appalling sound than they had ever heard, seeming like the mingled groans and shrieks of a million of damned souls in their agony of despair.

The three travellers plodded wearily onwards in silence, all secretly praying that the end of their journey might soon be reached, and cursing their evil stars for ever having rashly ventured upon such an expedition. All at once Mr. Wilkins, who was walking on a little ahead, stopped short, and called to them, in a tone of alarm.

"Look here," he said, "what are we to do? Here's a sort of bridge to cross over that might be just managed by a tight-rope dancer, but by nobody else, I should think."

The bridge in question was, indeed, an ugly construction to a nervous person not over sure of his footing. It was only the trunk of a tree, laid carelessly across a deep water-course, with a swollen stream rushing impetuously below.

With great circumspection, and some trepidation, Mr. Wilkins and Tom managed to get over to the other side, but half-way across the poor Doctor's foot slipped, and in a terror lest he should lose the cherished band-box, he overbalanced himself, and fell headlong into the frothing waters, the tree following, and, fortunately, falling wide of him.

CHAPTER XIII.

IN WHICH SOMEBODY MAKES A MISTAKE.

HAPPILY, in spite of the foam and splash it made, the stream the bridge crossed was not more than a foot or two in depth at the place where the Doctor had fallen. The water roared over some smooth granite blocks, but so strong was the current that a much heavier man might have been swept off his legs by it, and hurried down the gorge into an abyss beyond, down which the waters fell with a noise like distant thunder.

Still retaining his hold upon the bonnet-box, Doctor Griffin shouted loudly for help, as he was washed swiftly onwards, over the slippery stones, or hurled violently against the ragged edges of the rocks at the sides of the gorge. The darkness lending additional terror to this moment of peril, Tom and Wilkins ran wildly along the edge of the stream, leaping from rock to rock with desperate fearlessness, shouting loudly to the Doctor to catch at the end of the mountain-poles they held out to him.

The lantern Tom carried was of no service in this strait, for, at the first alarm, he had let it fall, and had kicked it away among the snow; but the quickly succeeding flashes of lightning blazing overhead brought every object out in vivid distinctness, showing for a moment the lowering peaks of the mountain above, standing in bold relief against the sky, and heavy masses of snow bearing down upon them from the heights above like a huge shroud.

In an interval of light the Doctor had seized upon the end of the stick Tom held out to him, and was endeavouring to scramble up the rocks, when Tom's feet slipping from under him, he, too, rolled down into the water, and floated swiftly towards the edge of the abyss, at a distance of about fifty yards. Nearer to this the channel was much narrower, and the water rushed down with more force. As he approached, Tom's notion was, "If I can get my legs across, I can block up the passage, and save us both."

By this time the poor Doctor's strength was almost gone. He had abandoned the bonnet-box to its fate, and was clutching frantically at the edges of the rocks as they slipped by him. Wilkins, meanwhile scrambling onwards, had bellowed himself hoarse with impossible advice, and was vainly endeavouring to push the end of the remaining pole within their reach.

In fact, the moment was one of imminent peril, and it seemed more than likely that both our travellers would be drowned, when, by some Providential chance, having by this time reached within six yards of the fall, they were simultaneously arrested in their downward course by being brought in sharp contact with a pole wedged across the passage, one of the two that had fallen in the water. This barrier stopping their headlong course, saved their lives. Tom, clutching at the rocks, dragged himself out of the water; whilst, at the same moment, Wilkins made good his hold upon the almost senseless Doctor, and hauled him up upon the snow, where he lay silent and motionless.

"Where's the lantern got to?" cried Tom, in trembling tones, for he was nearly dead with cold. "Is that it sticking out of the snow?"

It proved to be lying at the spot to which Mr. Kidd pointed, and Mr. Wilkins, with great difficulty, managed to re-ignite the damp candle-wick.

"If ever we get home again," the Doctor was then heard to mutter betwixt his chattering teeth. "If ever we get home again—oh, if ever!"

"I shan't try anything steeper than Primrose-hill in future," observed Mr. Wilkins. Let's get the old gentleman on his feet again before he freezes stiff to the rock."

" And the bonnet-box—the fatal bonnet-box," cried Tom; " it's done for this time, and no mistake."

But he was wrong; for, just at that moment, as sure as I am sitting here writing these lines, another lurid flash revealed the cause of so much of their sufferings, safely wedged between two rocks at twenty yards' distance; and Mr. Wilkins crawled on his hands and knees, and grasped it tightly.

" Don't you fall in, too," said Tom, in great alarm, pulling at his coat-tails.

They had no small difficulty in raising the Doctor on to his feet, and, with the aid of their brandy bottles, putting enough life into his exhausted frame to enable him to stagger feebly onward.

" There's something dark a little higher up," said Mr. Wilkins, " that I should say was a hut. We may help him that far, and then——"

But what was then to be done with the unfortunate gentleman was far from clear. The Doctor was scarcely alive. He was so much bruised, and so frightened, and well-nigh chilled to death by the icy coldness of the water into which he had been plunged. Tom was not much better, and his limbs trembled with cold as though he had got the palsy.

But they managed somehow half to crawl and half to stagger up to the object which Mr. Wilkins had pointed out, and which proved to be a low building, without a door, and entered by an arched opening. Mr. Wilkins went in first with the lantern, and the other two followed close upon his heels.

But at the first sight of the contents of the place, they all started back with an exclamation of surprise and alarm. It was the Morgue, or dead-house, where the bodies of those who perish upon the mountains are placed, when found, and a score of mummified figures, only half-decayed, with drooping jaws and sightless eyes, confronted them in horribly grotesque attitudes, as though they had been frozen stiff whilst dancing a " Can-can."

"For mercy's sake, let us get away from here," said the Doctor. "It's like going alive into one's tomb; for I am afraid I shall not live out the night."

"I hear a strange noise over there among the snow," said Tom. "It's some awful sort of wild beasts coming down upon us—a gang of wolves, perhaps. Aren't there wolves hereabouts?"

"I can't think of my natural history just at this moment," replied Mr. Wilkins, "but I vote we don't leave this shelter, although we have such ugly company. We're safer here; and see, there is some dry wood—we might, perhaps, light a fire."

As he uttered the last word, a deep, low baying smote upon the listeners' ears, which was audible above the din of the storm.

"That's nearer," whispered Tom. "The brutes have struck the scent."

"If they're on the other side of the gorge," said Wilkins, "the fallen bridge may save us. I hope to God it will, for we can't do much against them without fire-arms."

"We shall be worried like so many rats."

"We must make a fight for it. Hush! does not that sound nearer?"

There was no doubt of it. The sounds were rapidly approaching, and, horrible to relate, were not upon the other side of the gorge, as the travellers had hoped, but close at hand, upon the mountain-side.

Nearer and nearer they came, the same baying sound now swelling into a roar. The thick snow hid the noise of their feet, but during a momentary lull of the storm, in which the terrified fugitives listened with suspended breath, the silence of their enemies' approach seemed only to add terror to their coming.

"How awful!" said Tom, who, grasping a lump of wood he had picked up from the floor of the charnel-house, stood upon the defensive.

The Doctor only groaned. One can die only once, it occurred to him. After all, he might as well be worried as frozen to

death, and he was stupefied by the intense cold: he could not
thoroughly realize the danger threatening him.

Their friend was silent. He was waving to and fro the lantern
he carried at the entrance to the hut. Presently he burst out
laughing. Tom supposed, at first, that fear had turned his brain.

"Why, they are dogs," cried Mr. Wilkins, in wild delight.
"The Great St. Bernard dogs. What a fool I was not to think
of that before. There are men with lanterns. Don't you hear
them shouting, 'Hallo! hallo! hallo!'"

"Hola! hola!" responded a voice from the snow.

"We're saved!" cried Tom, falling on his knees to rouse the
Doctor. "Do you hear? it's the dogs come to find us."

"Where's the bonnet-box?" asked the Doctor, in a faint voice.
"I hope the wet has not spoilt it."

Thus, in days of old, have knights, hewn down in battle, clung
with dead fingers to the cherished banners in defence of which
they had lost their lives. Brave heart! he was surely to have his
reward. Such a devotion as he had shown passes not unheeded
by the loved one. This is not quite as ungrateful a world as
your sneering cynics would have us to believe. Women do not
take a life's sacrifice as a matter of course. The good, and virtuous, and long-enduring are happy in the end. While we are
away fighting with King Richard, and breaking our lances in
the good cause, my lady waits and watches for us from the turret of her father's castle, and does not console herself with the
society of other gallant knights, who stayed at home when we
went to the wars.

The dogs had now reached the spot. A huge, boisterous,
shaggy monster was licking the Doctor's face. Another placed
his paws on Tom's shoulder, and a third knocked Mr. Wilkins
backwards among the bones. Then three monks, carrying lanterns, came running up, shouting and out of breath, and with
difficulty called the dogs away.

The travellers' supply of brandy was exhausted, but their

deliverers produced some from a bottle, which they administered to the poor Doctor, and were presently able to get him upon his feet, and help him on. There was not very much more walking to be done before they came in sight of the convent, which was very fortunate, for the Elder Single Gentleman was by this time utterly exhausted, and almost unconscious.

The snow had obliterated all traces of the path by which they ought to travel, and, but for their guides, it would have been impossible for them to have found the way.

"We should have made three more in that horrible place," said Tom, glancing back at the dead-house with a shudder.

The monks told him that, in consequence of the intense cold, the bodies of the poor creatures found in the snow are preserved for a very long time before they gradually shrivel up and decay, and that the features of some had been known to be recognizable so long as three years after their death. Lying there in the dresses and attitudes in which they were found, there is something horribly ghastly about those silent figures, from which those familiar with death in other shapes will turn with a shudder.

Urged on by the prospect of warmth and shelter, Tom and Mr. Wilkins required little coaxing upon the road, and the monks helped the Doctor on between them. When they came at last in sight of the convent, the lights were gleaming bright from the windows over the snow; and when they approached, some other monks with lighted torches came out to welcome them. Some other dogs, too, came rushing forth, bounding and barking with every manifestation of joy, and would have knocked Mr. Wilkins down again, had not one of the monks providentially interposed.

"I feel like another prodigal son," said the funny gentleman, whose spirits had never been thoroughly depressed, even in the moments of greatest danger, and who had only ceased his joking out of consideration for the feelings of his two friends. "If I was only quite sure of always being found, I would come and do it every season."

It proved, however, upon inquiry that it was by no means too sure, as a general rule. During the winter-time, and upon other occasions when they think there is any necessity, the monks, accompanied by the dogs, go out at night in search of lost travellers; but it frequently happens—as the dead bodies testify—that some poor creature is overlooked. In this particular case, the party who had preceded the Two Single Gentlemen having reached the convent, had reported their coming, and as the evening wore on without their arrival, it had been thought advisable to go out in search of them.

Indeed, so great an event was their discovery by the dogs, that all the other visitors were in a state of tremendous excitement, awaiting their arrival.

" I wonder if we can get some dry clothes," said Thomas.

"Or shall we all have to go to bed till we're dry," suggested Mr. Wilkins; " let's ask one of these gentlemen."

" You can have a hot supper and a good fire," the monk explained, smiling; " and we can do something, too, in the way of a change of dress, but we cannot promise much about the fit."

About the fit. An unpleasant thought entered Thomas's mind. What sort of an appearance would he make before the pretty actress? And the Doctor—would he be able to appear at all. If not—Ha! ha! But he must hide his emotions and bide his time.

Why should I have to blush for my Younger Single Gentleman, whose adventures hitherto I have penned with pride and pleasure? How could he have become so unworthy of himself? How could he forget the tender care his friend and tutor of so many years' standing had bestowed upon him, and basely intrigue to cut that tutor out? Oh, love! most potent power, et cetera!—for which please see the poets. How base it will make the noblest among us! How low had my Thomas fallen under its baneful influence!

Arrived within the convent walls, Tom saw his tutor taken up to his bed-room, and comfortably tucked up in bed.

"I'm all right now," said the old gentleman, cheerfully.

"No, no, you're not," responded the deceitful Thomas.

"Oh yes, I am—as you say, as right as ninepence."

"Not at all, not at all."

"But I am, I say."

"But I say you're not."

"But what's the matter with me?"

"Why, everything. You're in an awful way. They all say so."

"Who's all?"

"Oh, everybody; one of the monks."

There are some people who never will believe they are in a bad way till they are screwed down in their coffins. It had been suggested that Tom also should be put to bed and kept there, in company with a hot-water bottle, for the next twelve hours, but Mr. Kidd was far too high-spirited a young man to submit to such treatment.

"It's all very well for the old gentleman," he said; "besides, he's really in a bad way. He is, indeed."

When Tom got up stairs into his warm bed-room he made a very singular discovery. Somehow, things seemed to dance unsteadily before his eyes, and the floor heaved towards him as though he had been aboard a ship in a storm. All the way up the mountain, after they were rescued, he had been saying to himself—

"When I get in-doors and have changed my clothes, won't I just eat a deuce of a dinner."

But, strange to say, now he had got in-doors he was not at all hungry. His head ached too, and he felt, when he had sat a few minutes before the fire, very hot, tired, and sleepy.

Suddenly a reason for all this occurred to him.

"It is that horrid brandy," he said; "I took such a lot coming up, and did not notice it when I was out in the cold. It is like those fellows who taste wine at the docks, who are as sober as judges until they go out into the streets."

He had taken off his wet clothes and put on a long night-shirt, and wrapped himself up in a blanket, to wait till a suit of clothes that some other visitor was going to lend him was brought upstairs.

TOM BEAUTIFIES.

"He is just your size," the monk had said, "and they will look as well as though they had been made for you."

These tidings cheered Mr. Kidd's heart.

I'm not such an awkward size to fit as the Doctor," he

thought; " I was almost afraid I should not have been able to see her until my own clothes were fit to put on."

The worst of it was, when Tom came to look at himself in the glass, he thought he never recollected looking so ugly. His eyes were swollen by the cold, and his nose was absurdly red.

THE QUEEN OF THE PIRATES (AT THE THEATRE).

He set to bathing his face in cold water, hoping thus to allay the inflammation, but on the contrary, it seemed to increase it.

" I never saw my hair look so horrible," he said, after brushing and combing it furiously for a quarter of an hour. There's a pair of curling-irons in the fire-place. Hanged if I havn't a good mind—why shouldn't I ?

He had an old *Galignani* in his pocket, and put his hair in paper. Sitting on the edge of the bed, he waved a candle to and fro, and amused himself in the looking-glass, and presently laughed in a silly way, without any particular reason.

"I really am rather drunk," he said, in a confidential sort of way, to the candle; "I won't deceive you, my young friend. I really am—"

He was also dreadfully sleepy.

"I'd give the world," he said, after a brief pause, "for forty winks. Merely forty: any more would overdo it. I've plenty of time. They're sure to be here with the clothes in a minute or two, then I'll tell them to call me in half an hour. By the way, what a while they are bringing the clothes. I had better lie down and wait for them. I'll close my eyes and rest them, but I won't go to sleep till they come."

He slept till morning.

The storm had passed away. It was a beautiful day. Tom's head-ache had gone too. He thought, as he hopped out of bed, that he never felt better or lighter-hearted.

But stay a minute! What had happened? Had he not slightly somehow overslept himself? Was he not to have joined the company overnight in the *Refectoire*? Had not somebody kindly lent him a suit of clothes, in which he was to have made a favourable impression on somebody's heart?

"Merciful powers!" ejaculated the unhappy young gentleman; "what have I been doing?"

Upon a chair by the door lay the suit of clothes which had been borrowed on his account. There they lay, neatly folded up; and the servant, when questioned, explained that he had knocked several times at the door, and finding that Monsieur was sleeping so soundly, thought it best not to wake him.

"Why, hang it all," began Thomas, in the English language.

But he said no more. What was the good of saying anything? What is the good of saying anything, generally? It is only your wealthy despots whose word is listened to. There are many thousands of poor creatures who go on talking till the end of time, and no attention is paid to them. It must be awfully delightful to be able to vociferate in a voice of thunder, "Off with his head!" but more delightful still to know that the head is "offed" according to order.

Poor Thomas! he had rather made a mess of it. The Doctor being out of the way, he would have been able without the least opposition to have carried all before him.

Out of the way. By the way, when he came to think of it, was he out of the way?

Perhaps he had recovered sufficient to go down stairs; who could say? Perhaps he had worn a monk's gown, and it might have proved becoming. Ladies have such strange fancies, and an actress too, above all others.

"Oh! what an awful fool I've been," cried Tom, in despair. "But it's no use talking of it now."

His own clothes were dry by this time, and then he dressed himself, beguiling the time his toilet occupied by recalling the image of the ever-lovely Follejambe, as she appeared in her butterfly hat, in her *vivandière* costume—as a swell of the period —as a *petit abé*—and, last of all, as Queen of the Pirates, on board her ship, the *Flâmme d'Enfer*.

When he had got himself up to his own satisfaction, he went down stairs. He certainly looked much better this morning: his eyes were not so swollen, and his nose not nearly as red.

"After all," said he, "I am rather glad she did not see me last night." But this, of course, was nonsense. What was done could not be undone.

There were a good many people assembled in the *Refectoire*, and he was welcomed with some little enthusiasm when it became known that he was one of the heroes of yesterday's adventure. The ever-lively Mr. Wilkins was there, as lively as ever.

"Hallo! my early worm," said he; "how do you find yourself by this time? We have been waiting for your account of your perils and dangers. If you had only managed to get up in time for the fireworks that were let off in your honour! We

H

put back the balloon till you came. We'll have that after breakfast."

Tom looked eagerly round the room.

" Are there no more ladies and gentlemen stopping here ?" he asked Mr. Wilkins, quietly.

" A great many have gone away this morning," replied his friend.

" Are all gone except those I see now ?"

" All but one lady."

Tom's heart fluttered.

" A young lady ?"

" Youngish old," said Mr. Wilkins; " or, more properly speaking, perhaps, ' oldish young.'"

" How do you mean ? She is pretty, is she not ?"

" Well, looked at in one way, in a certain light, perhaps. But she's got to be focussed carefully before you catch it."

At this moment the door opened, and the fair subject of the conversation entered the room. It was the celebrated Miss Strider, a literary pedestrian, who had been all over Europe on foot by herself, and who was fond of saying that she never yet had met with any one who endeavoured to molest her.

" It depends upon your own conduct, my dear," was what this lady remarked to a friend of the writer's. " A woman has only to thank herself for anything of that sort. One look is quite enough when it is properly done."

It is a charming idiosyncrasy of many young ladies that the outrageous male sex can be looked down and withered into the innermost depths of their unworthy high-lows. Then, again, there are many women to be found from whom, as Miss Strider said, one look *is* quite enough. This sort go through life easily, without meeting with any unpleasantness. There are others, again, with a different style of face, who cannot get to the street corner without being stared out of countenance. This, indeed, is strange, and requires thinking over quietly.

" But, I say," said Tom, " is there no one else ?"

" No one, I believe."

They made inquiries, and found that there were only two other travellers in the convent whom Tom had not seen. These were a married couple, of whom the lady, being indisposed, was keeping her room, and the husband had breakfasted and gone out very early in the morning.

Tom, without loss of time, sought out his friend and tutor. He found that gentleman making his toilet with great care, and smiled sarcastically.

" Have you seen Mademoiselle ?" asked the Doctor.

" Of course not."

" Not been down yet ?" This seemed to please the Elder Single Gentleman.

" Oh, yes, I have."

" She is not down then, I suppose ?"

" Well, I suppose she isn't. She's not here."

The Doctor's jaws fell open like a toy nut-cracker.

" Not here ?"

" Of course not."

" Been and gone ?"

" Never been. No one of the name of Follejambe ever been up the mountain."

The Doctor was silent for awhile.

" Let's go at once," said he. " This really is not treating us with proper courtesy."

" Oh ! I suppose we shall get another letter, fixing another rendezvous."

" No more of this folly," said Doctor Griffin, with decision. " Let us show her that we are not mere puppets, to be pulled all over Europe by a string."

" How can we show that if we don't see her. She writes a letter and flies away, and does not seem to care whether we get it or not."

" It is too ridiculous."

" It is rather ridiculous. However, for the future——"

" I suppose there could not have been an accident," said the Doctor, after a pause.

In less than two hours' time they were descending the mountain. Miss Strider was of their party, and had taken a great fancy to the Doctor. Apart to Mr. Kidd, she had observed,—

" What an extremely intellectual head your friend has !" It has been said, in a former portion of this history, that Doctor Griffin's phrenological development was intellectual to a fault: indeed, it was, if any thing, according to the opinion of Thomas's dear mother, " rather too bumpy."

The Elder Single Gentleman may, perhaps, have found some consolation for his wounded feelings in the society of Miss Strider, for they walked and talked together very amicably.

" It is so seldom," she was overheard remarking, " that one finds a mind capable of grasping one's meaning."

It would have been as well, perhaps, had our doctor of philosophy grasped more firmly instead the waist of the learned fair one, who, too venturesome at one portion of the descent, performed a summersault in the snow, and thereby brought to an unseemly conclusion a conversation of much brilliancy.

Two days afterwards, at Chamounix, there arrived, with their portmanteau, a letter from the faithless Follejambe. She was at the convent, she said. How was it they had gone away without seeing her ? She was indignant at their conduct, and wrote sharply. Then in a P.S. made another appointment.

" Thomas," said the Doctor, " this is all your blundering." Our two friends had almost a quarrel upon the subject.

" It was all that fool of a Wilkins ?" said Tom : " he made the inquiries."

" In _his_ French too," said the Doctor, bitterly. " No wonder they did not understand him."

That night Doctor Griffin had a strange dream. He thought he was again lost in the snowy wastes. Whilst wandering, he

heard cries of distress. It was the voice of his Follejambe
calling to him.   He found her upon the brink of an abyss, and
she fell over just as he stretched out his hand to catch her.
Somehow, having got down the abyss without hurting himself
he picked the dear one up, when lo! she changed to Miss Strider;
and at the same moment, three ridiculous geese and an absurd
baa-lamb came up and looked on, and said in chorus, Quack,
quack, and Ba-ba.   Then the Doctor awoke, and found his
shaving-water getting cold.

ANOTHER OF THE DOCTOR'S DREAMS.

CHAPTER THE LAST.

WHEREIN THE BONNET-BOX REACHES ITS DESTINATION.

OF course she was not there! It does not matter much where
"there" might have been. She was not to be found in the place

BAINS DE MER.

she had appointed, and once more our travellers were doomed to
be bitterly disappointed.

" What now ?" asked the Doctor.

" Let's go home again," replied Thomas ; and they turned their heads, with a groan, towards dear Old England.

But it was not to be their sad fate to leave France without another glimpse of the pretty actress. On their way home they stopped at a French bathing-place, and said the Doctor, " Let's have one day's enjoyment, if we can."

" I wish we'd gone to Ramsgate," said Thomas.

" Exactly what I advised, my dear boy."

"ARRETEZ ! ARRETEZ !"

" Oh, yes, I know. Don't begin all that again."
But the Doctor said no more. He felt hurt.

It was a glorious day by the sea-side, and all the dear, old sea-side business going on the same as ever. There were the loungers in their sand-shoes, and the mermaids sporting in the waves, and the wicked people with the telescopes.

" I've almost a good mind," said the Doctor, looking at the sea ; and, later on, he might have been seen travelling out into the ocean in a clumsy wooden carriage. Yet a little while and he might have been heard crying loudly to the driver to stop. " *Arretez donc*," he said, " *mes choses sont floater*. What do you

call it?—Look here—*la porte*—hang it, where are you going to?
I'm up to my waist in water."

But this little accident was soon forgotten in the excitement of
the news with which Thomas was awaiting his friend and tutor's
return to dry land.

ROCOCO AND HIS FAIR COMPANION.

"She's here," cried Thomas.   "I saw her just now out of the
hotel window."

"Where?"

"Walking with Rococo."

Somehow, it was not quite so pleasant to hear of Rococo. Yet
what did it matter? Who was Rococo? A mere nobody. She
had probably met him there at the sea-side, and he had forced his
stupid society upon her. Our Single Gentlemen found out, with-

out much trouble, the hotel where the Follejambe had put up, and
they sent in their cards:

Thomas Kidd.

WIDEAWAKINGTON.

Doctor Griffin.

Avec un Carton.

At the very last moment, after a series of the most artful
contrivances on the part of Mr. Kidd, the Doctor obtained
possession of the band-box, and kept a firm hold of it.

They found her waiting to receive them in a delightful boudoir,
where pink curtains flung a roseate tint upon her pretty face; but
somehow, she was not the Follejambe of those happy days gone
by, when De Rococo gave his famous supper-parties. She met
them indeed without a smile.

"I have brought the bonnet-box," said the Doctor.

"*Enfin!*" said she.

Enfin! At length! Was that to be all their reward for what
they had suffered on her account? Had they gone through a
hundred dangers to get at last no thanks—to be treated in this
way! Oh, WOMAN, WOMAN! There is no type in Mr. Ogden's

founts half large enough to brand thy perfidy, although he tells
me he can supply me with letters a yard square, if I desire them.
As our unhappy Single Gentlemen stood in the presence of this
cold-blooded syren, their hearts felt heavy and their throats full.

There were some explanations made, which the Two Single
Gentlemen listened to as in a dream. When Mr. Wilkins had
asked for the *danseuse*, at the convent, he had asked for the
name of Follejambe. He ought to have used another.

"I'll let her see, though," thought the Doctor, "that we can
get on pretty comfortably without her gratitude;" and he began
to compose a withering sentence. But she went on talking.

"I had quite given you up," she said, "you were so *very* long.
I waited, and waited. At last I gave the bonnet up, and was
MARRIED WITHOUT IT."

The room seemed to go round before the Doctor's eyes.
Thomas was speechless. Was the wedding she had talked about
going to her own? And who was the wretch—that is to say, the
happy man?

His name was De Rococo.

Somehow, on their way back to the hotel, the heroes of this
history avoided each other's eyes, and but little conversation
passed between them. It was not until an hour afterwards, in
the privacy of their sleeping apartment, that they found sufficient
courage to speak upon the subject nearest to their hearts. At
last, however, the silence was thus broken—

"Thomas," said the Doctor.

"Doctor," said Thomas.

"Does it not strike you, that when we submit a detailed state-
ment of our route and travelling expenses to your dear mother,
that—that—in fact—"

"That what?" asked Mr. Kidd.

"That it may occur to her, Thomas, we have been, as it were,
zig-zagging—I object to the too prevalent custom now-a-days of
coining words to save trouble, but you will, perhaps, allow it to

pass upon this occasion—that we have, then, been zig-zagging in rather an eccentric fashion?"

"We couldn't help it, could we?"

"Decidedly not, Thomas. No; decidedly, we could not help it."

"And we cannot help it now?"

"There is no doubt about that."

Well, then?"

"I beg your pardon!"

"'Well, then?' I said. In other words, what do you propose."

"I cannot say," replied the Doctor, after a few moments' reflection, "that I am exactly prepared with anything in the shape of a proposition. My ideas have not yet assumed any decided form; but I may go so far as to state that they tend towards something in the way of a judicious arrangement."

Is there any scene more melancholy than a deserted sea-coast in the evening time, when the golden glories of the setting sun fade into cold greys, and the deep shadows which have been hiding from the light beneath the overhanging cliffs, creep forth and spread over the sands; when the hoarse murmur of the coming sea is the only sound which breaks the silence; the dimly seen figure of a heavily laden fisherman, tramping wearily homewards, the only sight to vary the dreary monotony around?

Upon solitary coasts, ere now, sensitive souls have pined and fretted, and great hearts preyed upon themselves, waiting and watching for that which was never to come. I have done the same myself, at Clapham Junction, having taken the wrong turning in that maze of underground passages, and got upon the "down" side when I wanted the "up." Heaven help us! how often shall we be waiting on the down side as the up express rushes by unheeded? Some of us, mayhap, may still be found waiting on the wrong platform when the hour shall arrive for shutting up the station gates and turning out the lights. We patient, mistaken ones, are always up in good time—if anything a little too early. We take our stand (on the wrong platform) a good half-hour before the train is due (at the other platform) which we wish to travel by. It comes and goes, and we are left—upon the wrong side of the station.

These sage reflections were suggested to the writer by the touching account given to him of the Two Single Gentlemen strolling, sadly and silently, over the boulders and loose shingle of the sea-shore, on that dreadful evening after the Follejambe's

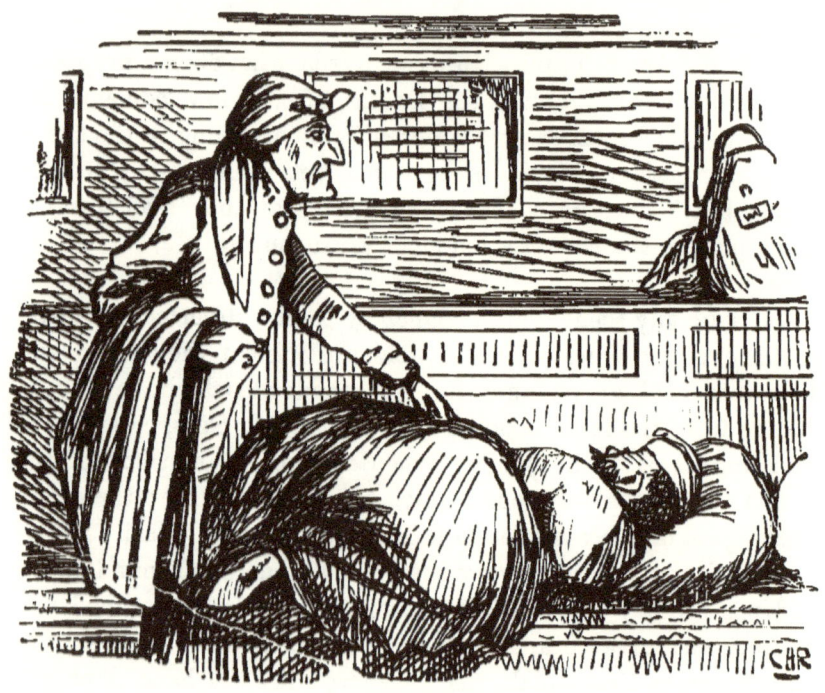

"S'IL VOUS PLAIT, THIS IS MY BERTH."

perfidy was revealed to them. It is a train of thought in which he occasionally indulges when looking from his cottage window across the Thames, on a rainy day, smoking a cigar. Then, reflecting how it had been his fate (alas!) to stand on the wrong side, he resolves to ——: but that is neither here nor there.

Oh, weary, weary time. Would the hour never come when *le paquetbot* should start for England. England, dear old England where all the women are true; where ballet-girls don't turn the heads of doctors of philosophy; where, in fact, such things

could not go on as, we know, had been going on any time these
last four weeks—of course not.

And, oh! what a passage that was which our travellers made
together across the briny deep, upon their way home to the
land of their birth! They were not inclined for much conversation, our two friends; and the Doctor, until a late hour, paced
the deck in pensive silence, and contemplated the moon. Presently the wind sprang up, and he sought his berth, which a
dreadful foreign person had taken the liberty of appropriating.

It was surprising how smoky dear old England looked, round
about the neighbourhood of London Bridge.

"Suppose," said Thomas, "we have a good drink of real old
English beer," and they entered the first public-house they came
to for that purpose. But they happened to sell bad liquor at this
establishment. Ah, me! the world is full of delusions. Nothing
is as it is said to be. Which of us is happy? Who is loved?
Who's who? What's what? And what does it all matter?

THE END.

www.ingramcontent.com/pod-product-compliance
Lightning Source LLC
Chambersburg PA
CBHW022139020726
47496CB00008B/2461